2008

Jan 2011

Love Finds You
in
Snowball
ARKANSAS

Love Finds You in Snowball ARKANSAS

BY SANDRA D. BRICKER

**Doubleday Large Print
Home Library Edition**

summerside
PRESS

This Large Print Edition, prepared especially for Doubleday Large Print Home Library, contains the complete, unabridged text of the original Publisher's Edition.

Love Finds You in Snowball, Arkansas
© 2008 by Sandra D. Bricker

ISBN 978-1-61664-954-8

All scripture quotations, unless otherwise indicated, are taken from the New King James Version®. Copyright © 1982 by Thomas Nelson, Inc. Used by permission. All rights reserved.

Scripture quotations marked NIV are taken from the HOLY BIBLE, NEW INTERNATIONAL VERSION®.

Cover photo by Marci Reno. Interior photos by Marci Reno and Mark Simmons.

Cover by Müllerhaus Publishing Group | **mullerhaus.net**

Published by Summerside Press, Inc., 11024 Quebec Circle, Bloomington, Minnesota 55438

Fall in love with Summerside.

Printed in the USA.

For D.

....

"Love . . . bears all things, believes all things,
hopes all things, endures all things.
Love never fails."
1 Corinthians 13:4, 7–8

Special thanks and honorable mentions
to my girls,
Jemelle, Marian, Debby, Loree, and Page,
who also never fail me.
And to Rachel, the best editor there is.

IF YOU BLINK WHILE YOU'RE LOOKING AT an Arkansas map, you could miss Snowball altogether. Perched right in the middle of Searcy County, Snowball was once a commercial center; however, when transportation improved in the 1950s, business moved to nearby Marshall. The Snowball school and post office closed down within ten years, and current-day "downtown Snowball" consists of little more than an old town meeting hall and the shell of a general store. The surrounding area is dotted with rustic and historic cabins and campsites, and some of the most beautiful scenery in the country revolves around the remarkable Ozarks region. An old adage about the area proclaims, "It's not that the mountains are so high; it's just that the valleys are so deep." The exquisite Buffalo National River, which runs through the area, is approximately 150 miles long and has both swift-running and placid sections. Deer and elk graze along its banks, and some of the best bass fishing in the region can be found there.

Sandra D. Bricker

Good morning, Lord!
   I promised myself when I started
this prayer journal that I wouldn't let
it turn into a whine-fest in ink. I really
tried to keep that promise, too. I mean,
I've thanked You daily for my stellar
job and for Mattie and for that day
when I stumbled upon the clearance
sale on work clothes at Macy's. And
I've certainly been appreciative of the
great hair days when they happen. But
I hope You'll forgive me as I digress
this morning because I just don't think
the numbers should be working

against me like they are. Case in point: There are roughly 200,000 people in the naked city of Little Rock, Lord. I figure 50 percent of them are male. If you take away half of those as married or involved—and probably another quarter who are either gay or just not worth the effort—that should still leave a few good options from which to choose, right?

Well, where are they? Seriously. Are they hiding? Out of town? Living in Tucson? My thirtieth birthday is looming on next month's horizon like a giant meteor barreling toward Earth, and I'm starting to wonder if this will just be another decade in the pursuit of great hair and Friday nights at the movies with Matt. Don't get me wrong, I'm really thankful for all my blessings, and I'm not asking for a parting of the Red Sea here or that You turn someone into salt or anything. I'd just like to meet one average someone. [Well. You know. Not TOO average.] Someone who will cherish me and appreciate me. Someone who will share my life with me.

Not that there's too much life left now, of course. I mean, I'll be 30 next month, Lord. I know You already know this, but I thought I'd just remind You. I'm not getting any younger here.

Love,
Lucy

Chapter One

"I TELL YOU, I'M SAILING UP THE RELATIONSHIP river with a broken rubber paddle and a slow leak in my boat!" Lucy told her best friend, Matt Frazier, as they inspected the goodies on the snack table at the back of the room. "I mean, what is the deal here? I know I'm no Paris Hilton—"

"Thank You, Lord."

"Ah, thanks, Mattie," she said with a grin as she lifted a Danish with the wrong end of a plastic spork. "What is this?"

"Pineapple, I think."

Lucy's upper lip twitched on one side as she dropped the thing back to the plate and moved on to a tray of mystery roll-ups.

"Cream cheese?"

"I hope so."

"Anyway, I'm no blond bombshell," she continued. "But I've got other good points, don't I?"

"Indeed you do."

"I'm reasonably attractive."

"A solid nine."

"Really, Mattie? A nine?

"Solid."

Lucy smiled, happy with the rating. "I'm intelligent."

"A good, hearty . . . five."

"Hey."

"Kidding. You're a Rhodes scholar waiting to happen."

"You bet I am," she replied after a chuckle. "And I have this great French genealogy going on."

"*Vous êtes magnifique*," he stated with flair.

"Matt. You speak French?"

"Only what I remember from four years of it in high school. *Continuer*," he urged with the motion of one hand as he poked a toothpick through a meatball with the other.

"I'm tolerably fit and in good health. Oooh! And some days, I have really great hair," she stated with determination.

"You really do."

"So what's the deal? Why am I still single and alone?"

"I don't know," he replied and then plopped the meatball into his mouth, talking over it. "But it's wrong in any language."

"I know."

Lucy looked down at a messy stack of flyers on the table nearby.

RELAX. RENEW. REFRESH.
SEEK HIS WILL FOR YOUR LIFE.
JOIN THE SINGLES MINISTRY IN SNOWBALL, ARKANSAS,
FOR A WHOLE WEEK OF PRAYER, PRAISE, AND FUN.

"What do you think about this?" she asked Matt.

"I was going to ask you. I think it would be a ton of fun. Alison said they were planning a fishing trip, maybe some kayaking."

"Oh, right up my alley," Lucy remarked. "Not."

21

"C'mon, kiddo. Let's sign up."

"You feel free," Lucy told him. "If I'm going on a retreat to relax and renew, it's going to be at a four-star hotel somewhere overlooking a beach."

She didn't want to say it out loud, but there was also the company they would be forced to keep. She loved the singles group, for the most part. But a whole week with them?

Lucy's lips slowly turned downward as she looked around the room at the singles gathered there. There were half a dozen people that Lucy didn't remember by name, people who had joined the group in the last few months as church membership grew. And then there were the regulars, the ones who were there rain or shine on the third Friday night of every month, for each of the five years since Lucy had joined the fellowship at Grace Community Church.

Alison Duncan. Thirty-five. A little bossy sometimes, but only because she's eager to create good experiences for the singles group.

Jeff Burnett. Forty-ish. Prematurely silver. Computer geek. Can be a little

SANDRA D. BRICKER

gruff, but there's a teddy bear waaaaay underneath.

Tony Howland. Under thirty, but not by much. Nice-looking. A little over-enthusiastic about things that don't really warrant it, but enthusiasm can't really be a bad thing.

Brenda Marco. A forty-something force of nature with her finger on the pulse of the church social scene. Brenda is tabloid television incarnate.

Cyndi Llewellyn—

Lucy's thoughts came screeching to a halt as her eyes landed on six feet of rugged, luscious potential boyfriendness as HE sauntered through the door. Straight blond hair that brushed the collar of his denim shirt. A square jaw shadowed in light stubble. Broad shoulders. Amazing green eyes.

"Who. Is. That?"

Matt gave the doorway a casual glance and then turned his attention to the chicken wings he'd just piled on a paper plate.

"Oh, that's Justin Something. He joined last month."

"Justin What?"

"I can't remember. Nice guy.
Contractor. Owns his own company."

"He looks like that underwear model in
the Macy's commercials." Lucy's eyes
rounded as the "model" approached, and
she full-on grinned when he extended his
hand toward Matt.

"How are you, Matt?"

"Great, Justin. Good to see you again,"
Matt replied, wiping his hands on a
napkin before completing the handshake.
"This is my friend Lucy Binoche."

"Justin Gerard," the vision said to her.

"Lucy." *Matt already told him, Lucy.
Don't repeat yourself like a dork.* "Lucy
Binoche." *Will you stop it?*

"So are you two going on the retreat to
the Ozarks?" he asked, oblivious to the
fact that his green eyes were piercing a
hole right through Lucy.

Matt was quick to reply. "Nah."

"I'm sorry to hear that. I thought it might
be fun," he told them, running a hand
through his streaks-of-light hair.

"You're going?" Lucy's heart began to
race.

"I am. In fact, I'm going over to sign up
right now."

"Me, too," she told him.

Matt squinted at her. "I thought you said—"

"I think it will be fun," Lucy interrupted. "Come on, Matt. Join us."

"Really." Matt was completely deadpan. "And here I thought you weren't interested in log cabins and trout fishing."

"Smallmouth bass, actually," the vision interjected. "You'd have to go up to White River for the trout experience. Buffalo National is bass territory."

"I love a good sea bass," Lucy said, reminding Matt of something he already knew.

"Well, I don't think smallmouth bass are exactly what you're thinking of," Matt told her.

Grilled sea bass was the special the last time they'd eaten at Loca Luna. It had come with buttermilk mashed potatoes and cream gravy, along with a perfect serving of steamed vegetables.

"Oh. I know that. I was just joking."

"Well, come on, Matthew. Put your name down," Justin prodded, and then he turned toward the sign-up table at the far end of the room.

As they followed, Matt drew loony circles around his ear at Lucy. "You're nuts," he mouthed without a sound.

"Oh, be quiet," she mouthed back at him. "He's *gooooorgeous!*"

* * * * *

Lucy had been running Guest Services at the Conroy Hotel for nearly six years. Not one day had passed when she didn't think of a reason to love her job. The Conroy was the first five-star boutique hotel in Little Rock. The lobby alone made it worthwhile to come to work with its well-placed antique furniture, round marble fireplace, and unexpected pops of color. The rooms were understated and elegant; each contained a four-poster queen bed draped in panels of silk.

The phone was ringing as Lucy walked into her office, and Lois, the administrative assistant, answered with a velvet voice.

"Guest Services. How may we serve you today?"

Lucy's desk was partitioned off from the rest of the office, and behind the slate blue cubicle sat an impressive mahogany desk, several filing cabinets, and a

credenza in a matching wood grain.
Two wine-colored wingback chairs flanked
the desk on either side, upholstered in
soft micro-suede. The crystal bowl of
potpourri and three pillar candles on the
credenza gave the office a sweet vanilla
kiss.

She'd just dropped into her dark brown
leather chair when Lois called to her from
the other side of the room.

"Morning."

"Morning."

"Matt can't make lunch until one
o'clock. And the VIPs in the Presidential
Suite are looking for tickets to the
Shakespearean festival on Saturday."

"Is Matt in his office?"

"Only until nine thirty."

"I'm going to take a walk down to
Bookkeeping. Will you call on those
tickets?"

"You got it."

"Thanks, Lois."

Lucy smoothed her navy blue pencil
skirt with the palm of her hand as she
stepped into the elevator and pressed the
button for the lobby. When the doors
closed, she used the reflection of the

shiny golden walls to fluff her long dark-red curls and straighten the collar of her starched white blouse.

"Consider it part of your job description," the general manager of the hotel had announced at the last meeting of the service staff. "Once you enter the lobby of this hotel, there should not be a visible wrinkle or a hair out of place. When representing the Conroy, you are each responsible to do so in a professional and elegant manner, in keeping with this hotel's five-star personality."

The *click-click-click* of Lucy's three-and-a-half-inch heels against the cold, polished marble of the lobby floor kept a perfect rhythm as she smiled and nodded to each guest and staff member she passed.

Down the hall and to the left . . . It was only nine in the morning, yet Matt already looked as if he'd worked a full day. His sandy brown hair was tousled, and his tie hung loosely around his neck. His sport coat was spread across the credenza behind his desk, and his shirtsleeves were rolled to the elbow.

"Hey, what are you doing down here?" he asked when he saw her. He slipped the wire frames from his face and tossed them to the desk. "Slumming a little bit?"

"Just a little bit," she replied. "I wanted to find out if you're mad at me."

"You know better than that." Matt's hazel eyes twinkled. "You mean because of the about-face on the Ozarks trip?"

"Yeah."

"Not mad. Just reminded."

"Of?"

"Of how unstable you really are."

"Oh, that. Yeah. Sorry."

"Hey, if you remember, I was the one who wanted to go on the trip to begin with. You, my friend, are the one who said it wasn't worth our time."

"That was before God dropped my new boyfriend into the picture."

"Your boyfriend already? He certainly does move fast."

"Not yet," Lucy admitted. "But I plan to inspire him out in Snowball."

"Snowball? That's where we're going?"

"Some retreat camp of log cabins and hiking trails. Near that Buffalo place."

"Buffalo National River?"

"Right. There."

"And you'll be hiking on this trip, will you?" Matt asked her, his skepticism blinking like an electrical sign with a short.

"I certainly will. Hiking, fishing, rowing something."

"I can hardly wait to see this."

"I'm glad to hear it," she said mischievously. "Because I'm going to bring Chinese food over to your place tonight, and you're going to teach me how."

"How to what?"

"Fish. And row."

Matt burst into laughter and then nodded.

"It's a date, Lucy. Don't forget the crab rangoon, and I'll teach you how to row something."

"Deal."

On her way to the elevator, the front desk manager handed her two pink message slips to review in the ride back up to the mezzanine.

THE PALMERS, RM 420. WANT YOUR RECOMMENDATION FOR A DINNER RESERVATION. HUNGRY FOR SEAFOOD.

FLOWERS DELIV'D TO GOVERNOR'S SUITE, PER
YOUR INSTRUX. CARD READ: WELCOME BACK. LUCY
IN GUEST SERVICES.

There was nothing Lucy loved more than making a guest experience memorable, and she'd developed quite a reputation for doing just that.

She picked up her desk phone and dialed before she even sat down. "Mrs. Palmer, it's Lucy Binoche in Guest Services. I'm going to make a reservation for you and Mr. Palmer at a place called The Terrace. They have a sea bass on the menu that's exquisite. What time would you like to have dinner?"

"Lucy, you're a treasure. How about seven thirty?"

"Sounds great. You'll want to leave the hotel by seven, and I'll leave directions for you at the front desk."

"What would we do without you? I wish we could take you home with us."

"Careful, I might sneak into your luggage," Lucy teased. "Now, you have a wonderful dinner. And be sure to order the raspberry crème brûlée for dessert. It's unforgettable."

"Oooh, that sounds perfect. It's our anniversary, you know."

"Your anniversary?" she exclaimed. "That's wonderful!"

"Forty beautiful years."

"Congratulations, Mrs. Palmer. As a single girl myself, I find forty years awe-inspiring."

"You're still single, Lucy? What a shame that some man doesn't have any idea how much he's missing. But you'll find him, sweetheart. You can be sure of that."

"From your lips to God's ears," she added. "Have a lovely celebration."

"We will."

People always marveled that she was still single, and Lucy took a moment to marvel a bit herself. Then, remembering Justin and the upcoming retreat to Snowball, she shook her head and smiled.

"Lois, have an arrangement delivered to the Palmers in four twenty. Something elegant. Something by Preston Bailey. Maybe an Enchantment bouquet."

"Card?"

"Best wishes on your fortieth.

Compliments of your friends at the Conroy."

"Champagne?"

"No. Mr. Palmer is insulin-dependent and on blood pressure medication."

"How do you remember that?"

Lucy lifted one shoulder in half a shrug. "I just do."

"Okay," Lois said with a laugh. "You got it."

"I'm going down to the lounge for a while. We've got English high tea for the Braxton bridal shower this afternoon, and I just want to make sure everything is on track before the mother of the bride's plane arrives."

I love my job, Lord!

This week, the Palmers were back to visit. I always love it when they come to Little Rock. The Braxtons are having their daughter's bridal shower in the lounge, and the mayor's surprise party will be held in the ballroom at the end of the month. That's going to mean lots of VIPs coming to town, all of them looking for something special from Guest Services. Thank You so much for planting me at the Conroy. For the first time in my life, I feel like I'm doing exactly what I'm meant to be doing.

In my work life anyway.

What am I meant to be doing in my romantic life? Is Justin Gerard the answer to that prayer? He makes my heart pound and my palms sweat and my knees grow weak, but does that mean he's The One for me?

I have such a good feeling of anticipation about this trip to Snowball. Like some of my questions are bound to be answered there. Alison's flyer advertised this retreat as an opportunity to seek Your will for our lives, and that's what I really want to do. I want to put my best foot forward with Justin and see if we click—that is, if You let me know my feeling about him is right.

But just remember it's me, Lord. Sometimes I get caught up in my own thoughts and I miss what You're trying to say to me.

So You'll have to talk veerrry sloooowly and VERY LOUDLY to make sure I don't miss the point.

Listening already,
Lucy Louise Binoche

Chapter Two

"I DON'T GET IT. YOU'RE FISHING THE BUFFALO and you don't want me to come along?"

Matt set down the can of raw almonds and turned toward his friend, only to find him fiddling with the fishing pole Matt had left propped up against the refrigerator.

"Put that down," he said, snapping it out of George's hand.

"I'm just checking it out."

"You break everything you touch, Sedgewick," Matt teased.

"Is that why you don't want me to come along? Afraid I'll break something? Come on. What are you making, anyway?"

"Trail mix," Matt replied, returning his attention to the ceramic bowl on the counter. "For the trip."

"What's in it?"

Matt gave George an elbow just in time to keep George's hand out of the bowl. "Raw almonds, raisins, pumpkin seeds. Virtually nothing that you'd enjoy."

"I see a bag of chocolate chips there," George declared. "I like chocolate chips."

"Those are for Lucy."

"Lucy?" he exclaimed, incredulous. "Lucy is going, but you don't want me along?"

"It's a church retreat for the singles group, Sedgewick. There will be Bible verses and worship singing and lots of Jesus talk."

"Oh."

"Still want to go?"

"Will any of the females be as hot as Lucy?"

"Shut it . . ."

"Why won't you set me up with her, Frazier?" George asked sincerely, snatching up the bag of chips and pouring a few into his mouth. "You two are just friends, right?"

"The best."

"Then why can't I take a pass at her?"

Matt withdrew his hands from the bowl and glared at George. "The very fact that you chose those words to express your desire to date my friend is the reason you're never going to."

George dumped a few more chips into his mouth before Matt took the bag away from him and emptied the rest of them into the bowl.

"Seriously," he said to Matt. "Why haven't you and Lucy ever hooked up?"

Matt lifted one shoulder into a shrug. "Growing up, she was Lanie's friend."

"So? I tried to date every friend my sister ever had."

"I've known her since she was six, Sedgewick," Matt replied. A nostalgic smile crept over his face. "I took her to a dance once when she was a freshman, but only because her date left her in the dust at the last minute. Lanie and her date are there, and Lucy is there, all dressed up in this frilly pink number, and the guy just bails on her. Never shows up."

"Ah, man."

"I know. So I spend all night working up the courage to kiss her. After the dance, we're standing on her front step, and just as I'm about to make my move, she goes into this speech about how she's always wanted a brother and how great it is that she has me. After that, I guess it was only natural for me to remain a sort of fraternal figure to her."

"That still doesn't tell me why I can't—"

"Well, you can't," Matt interrupted.

"So, what? There will be fishing on this trip? And what else?"

"The usual outdoor rituals," Matt told him, turning the trail mix a few times with both of his hands.

"Hiking. Boating."

"Yeah."

"And I can't go—why again?"

"It's the singles group only this time around. But if you'd go to church with me now and then, you'd be invited to these extravaganzas."

"High price to pay for some camping out."

"Sedgewick, why are you here?" Matt asked with a grin.

George thought for a moment, and

then he jumped as if bitten by a sudden current of electricity.

"Oh, right. I've got Razorback tickets."

"For when?"

"Tonight."

"In Fayetteville?"

"Yeah. If we take off right now, we can make the second quarter."

Matt portioned out trail mix into several small plastic containers and popped on the lids.

"I'm not driving almost three hours each way for a basketball game tonight, George."

"You got something better going on?"

"I've got dinner with Lucy."

"Of course you do." George snatched up the fishing rod again and shook it at his friend. "Catching it first?"

"Something like that."

"Come on, Frazier. Come with me."

"You'd better get on the road if you want to make the second quarter."

"You're no fun."

"What can I say? You know me."

"Yes, and it's quite the burden, let me tell ya."

"Leaving so soon?" Matt asked him.

George laughed on his way out of the kitchen. "Have fun singing 'Kumbaya' around the campfire," he called from the front door.

"Oh, I will."

Matt was relieved when the door slammed behind George. They'd been the best of buddies since college, but George never did get the side of Matt that hungered for a deeper truth. He'd been hoping to pass that understanding to his friend for many years now, but somehow it just never clicked. Matt continued to pray that someday it would.

He checked his watch. There should be time to make a run to Lenny's Bait & Tackle before Lucy arrived with the Chinese food.

Grabbing a handful of trail mix from one of the containers, Matt jogged out the back door.

* * * * *

Lucy slipped into her favorite designer tee, a gray-and-white-striped number in the softest Egyptian cotton. She'd gotten it on sale at thirty percent off, but Matt loved teasing her about owning a tee shirt that had to be dry-cleaned.

She dialed the phone while zipping up her vintage denim jeans and stepping into chunky sandals that showed off her iced cinnamon toenails.

"I'd like to place a takeout order," she told the voice on the other end of the phone. "We'll need a pork lo mein, a cashew chicken with fried rice, and two eggrolls. Oh! And an order of crab rangoon. It's Lucy Binoche. I'll be there to pick it up in fifteen minutes. Thanks so much."

Tucking her cell phone into the green hobo bag she'd bought on eBay, Lucy snagged her keys from the brass hook by the door and hurried out.

"Give a girl a fish and she'll eat for a day," Lucy exclaimed the moment Matt opened his front door. "But *teach* a girl to fish, and she'll come home with a hot boyfriend named Justin."

Matt stood in the doorway, shaking his head.

"Lemme in."

"If you didn't have Chinese food in your hand, I might not."

Holding the bag up toward him, she began to swing it to and fro. "Mmmm," she teased. "Crab *rangooon*."

"Lucy Louise Binoche, you're lucky I'm starving."

The two friends discussed their workdays over dinner, exchanging barbs and anecdotes, plans and challenges. Hardly a minute passed in silence. They never seemed to run out of things to say to each other, and Lucy loved it that way. Matt was, without a doubt, her best friend in all the world.

"Mattie, you're such a good guy. I really appreciate your doing this."

"Doing what?"

"Helping me not to make a fool of myself."

"Well, you may be overestimating my abilities here, Luce."

"Come on," she said on a serious note. "I mean it. I just don't want to look like a total rookie out there."

"Would that be so bad?" he asked her. "I mean, you *are* a rookie. It doesn't change anything about who you are."

Lucy squeezed Matt's arm. "You don't understand."

"Nope. Guess I don't."

"Okay, so what's first?" she asked as

she hopped up and rinsed her plate in the sink. "Boating or fishing?"

When she returned to the dining room, Matt was standing in the middle of the adjoining living room, one brow arched and holding a fishing rod with both hands.

Lucy hurried toward him and reached for the pole.

"Not so fast," Matt chided. "First things first. Bait and Hook 101."

Lucy let herself sink down into the overstuffed chair facing the coffee table, and Matt sat on the sofa across from her.

"Buffalo National River is known for its smallmouth bass fishing," he explained, and he laid the pole to rest across his legs before opening a small white container. "And these, my friend, are like crab rangoon for bass."

Lucy looked down into the container and let out a one-syllable scream. "Mattie, what is that?"

"Worms, silly."

She grimaced and pressed herself against the back of her chair.

"Well, what did you think you were going to catch them with? Your good looks and charm?" Matt asked her. "Now come over here so I can show you how to bait your hook."

"Oh, Mattie. You're kidding, right?"

"Do you want to learn to fish or not?"

Their eyes locked for a long moment while she thought it over and worked to hold down her dinner. Finally, with a groan, Lucy got up and rounded the table, sitting on the edge of the sofa with guarded caution.

"You take them between your fingers like this," he demonstrated, and Lucy closed her eyes and turned away.

"Arrrrgh."

"You try."

"Matt, I can't."

"You can."

"I can *not*."

"Okay. It's no skin off my toes if you don't want to learn to fish after all. It's probably better that way anyhow. I mean, you were sure to make a complete fool of yourself."

"Oh, give it to me."

She clutched the squirming thing between two fingers, holding it away from her like a smelly diaper. Suddenly, the worm wiggled right out of her grasp and fell to the floor. Lucy hopped to her feet, screaming, and did a little dance as she jumped from one foot to the other and back again.

Matt leaned over and picked up the worm, and then he stared at her.

"Okay. Sorry."

Once she was seated again, he placed it between her two twitching fingers.

"Now you take the hook like this," he said, showing her, "and you pierce the worm once here, and then again here."

"Are you serious?"

"What do you mean?"

"You stab him? Twice? Why twice? Isn't once enough, Matt?"

"Twice. To keep the worm on the hook."

"Does it hurt him?"

"Maybe," he told her truthfully. "But not as much as being eaten by a bass, which is the overall plan, isn't it?"

Lucy looked at him with serious regard, and Matt burst out laughing.

"It's the circle of life, Lucy. You stab the worm and the fish eats the worm so that you can eat the fish."

"Oh, dear."

"Come on. Give it a try."

Lucy held the worm in front of her and leaned in toward it. "I'm so sorry," she whispered, and then she made several attempts before the hook finally went through the twisty-turny worm.

"One more time," Matt encouraged her.

"It's awful," she whimpered.

"I know. The things we do for love."

She tried several more times to make the second stab, but she just couldn't manage it.

"Okay, Mattie. I've got the idea. I don't have to torture him anymore, do I?"

Without a word, Matt removed the worm from the hook and tossed it back into the container. He then removed the hook from the end of the line.

"How about we try some casting?"

"Like throwing the line?" she asked, not quite containing her excitement. "Did you see that Robert Redford–Brad Pitt movie about the river and the fishing? It was so beautiful. They were out there in the middle of the river, throwing their fishing lines back and forth, back and—"

"Not in my living room!" Matt warned,

yanking the fishing rod away from her. "In the backyard."

A few dozen cast attempts later, the only injuries were sustained by a hanging ivy plant on Matt's patio and by a stray cat, who was appalled when it was unexpectedly slapped with the end of a fishing line.

Deciding to move on to the second lesson of the evening, they filed back into the house. It took both of them to lift Matt's prized kayak from the brace on the wall. Five minutes after they set it down in the center of the living room floor, Matt returned from the kitchen with two glasses of water on the rocks to find Lucy in the center of the kayak, swaying from side to side and feigning vertigo.

"The rapids through your living room are killer!" she cried, holding on to the sides of the craft with both hands. "I hope I can make it."

"I hate to rain on your adventure, Lucy, but with the weather conditions we've been having this fall, we may barely have enough water to float down the Buffalo National River."

"Aw, really?" she asked—but she didn't

know if she was really all that disappointed. "Then I'll just have to ride the current here at your place."

She let out the start of an overdone, stammering scream and then began to fight against her imaginary white-water current once again. She slammed against one side of the kayak and then the other and then back again.

"Whooops!" Lucy shouted suddenly as she tumbled onto the carpet, the overturned kayak resting in her lap and the glass of water Matt had brought her emptied over one leg and down the side of the table.

"Sorry."

"Only you, Lucy Lou," Matt commented. He sat on the arm of the sofa and gulped down his own glass of water. "Only you could turn over a kayak in the middle of the living room and all but drown in a glass of water."

* * * * *

Lucy always looked forward to Sunday mornings. She liked to attend the early service because that was when the choir performed. Many of the younger members of the church waited until the eleven o'clock service when the music was more contemporary, set off by guitars and drums and tambourines, but Lucy enjoyed the traditional hymns and the enormous pipe organ. She also liked the early service because that was when attendees were greeted just inside the double doors by Mr. and Mrs. Gamble, two of the original members of Grace Community Church and the first couple to be married there nearly fifty years ago. There was something so sweet and nurturing about them, and they always greeted her with a hug and a smile.

Pastor Dan's sermons were consistent in their uplifting and thought-provoking messages. This particular Sunday he recounted the life of Peter, a personal favorite of Lucy's. Peter was impetuous and impulsive; a bit of a slow learner but filled with childlike, hopeful faith. Although imperfect in every way, Peter was changed by meeting and sharing an intimate relationship with the Son of God. He later taught Christians about the sufficiency of God's grace, and yet he was a man who needed it more than most.

Leaning over toward Matt, Lucy whispered, "I'm definitely feeling Peter."

Matt grinned. "I hear you."

After the service, Lucy spotted Justin in the courtyard with Cyndi and Jeff from the singles group. Cyndi waved her over, and Lucy silently thanked her for it.

"We're headed to the Laughing Moon for brunch," Cyndi told her. "Do you want to join us?"

"That sounds great. I'll get Matt," Lucy replied. Trying to sound casual and feeling like she was failing in a big way, she added, "Justin, are you coming?"

"I am," he said, and the way he smiled at her turned her legs to warm jelly.

Those are the greenest eyes I've ever gone swimming in.

"I've got to drop Alison off at home," Cyndi told them. "I'll meet you there."

The Laughing Moon Café was one of Lucy's favorite Little Rock hangouts, just perfect for brunch after Sunday services. It was a bit of a drive from the church out to the historic Hillcrest neighborhood, but it was well worth the time for exceptional gourmet coffees, wonderful omelettes and quiches, customized pizzas and calzones, and an array of options for the most discriminating sweet tooth.

"So I heard that you and Matt have decided to join us on the retreat," Brenda Marco commented after they were all seated and dressing their various choices of coffee.

"Yeah, I think it will be a good time," Lucy replied, tearing open a packet of sweetener and emptying it into her café au lait.

"What about Lanie? Is she coming, too?"

"Nah," Lucy answered.

"Traveling?"

"Like always."

Lanie's job as a corporate trainer kept her between airports, rental cars, and hotels most of the time. Aside from picking up the luggage she'd borrowed from Lanie that week, Lucy hadn't spent any time with Matt's sister for a solid month.

When Brenda didn't speak again, Lucy glanced over to find her friend's expression glazed, her lips parted slightly, and her brown eyes fixed on Justin, who had the chair across the table from her.

"Yo. Bren."

Brenda blinked hard and then looked Lucy in the eyes and started to laugh.

"I'm sorry," she said at last and then lowered her voice. "He's handsome, isn't he?"

"Justin?" Lucy asked, trying not to overdo the innocent routine. "Yeah, I guess he is."

"Cyndi told me he's new in Little Rock. Moved here from North Carolina."

"That explains the slight drawl."

"Apparently he's quite the outdoorsman," Brenda continued. "Thirty-one years old, never been married. Tony says he's ready to settle down, though, and he's looking for someone real. That's what he said, I guess. Someone real. Doesn't want a woman too into her looks or too made up or high-maintenance. That counts me out, I suppose. Somebody at home on a campground, who can cook a good meal—"

"What, did he fill out a dating questionnaire?"

"I'm just telling you what I know," Brenda defended.

As much as Lucy appreciated getting

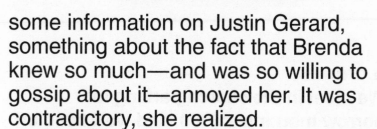

some information on Justin Gerard, something about the fact that Brenda knew so much—and was so willing to gossip about it—annoyed her. It was contradictory, she realized.

But still.

As Matt folded into the chair on the other side of her, Lucy looked down at her own outfit, skimming all the way down to the pink wedges she had gotten for a steal the week before.

"Do you think I'm overdressed?" she whispered to Matt.

"What do you mean? No."

She considered his reply for a moment and then sighed. Suddenly, she leaned back toward him once more and asked, "Do you think I'm high-maintenance?"

"Definitely," he replied. "More coffee?"

Hi, Lord.

We meet in the church parking lot tomorrow morning at 7:00, and we'll head off in two different cars for a place called Snowball. It's supposed to be pretty rural there, with dirt roads and log cabins. I'm imagining something like I once saw in a profile on Court TV, with rabid, wild animals and a scary backwoods yeti guy who peers through windows and plots his attack on visiting city girls.

I know. I need to stop watching those things, starting right now.

I was wondering if maybe You sent Justin Gerard to our singles group as an answer to my boyfriend prayers. He's a hottie, he's a Christian, he owns his own business, AND he's supposedly looking for a girlfriend. How perfect is he? I'm going to thank You right now for sending him and ask You to help me not make an idiot of myself in the woods.

Aside from that concern, I'm pretty much ready to go. I've got vacation time from work processed and approved. I stowed my Louis Vuitton and packed my things in a leather satchel and backpack I borrowed from Lanie. I've bought a fresh supply of chocolate and Oreos in case of emergency and some non-designer utilitarian clothes that are still cute enough to make Justin take a second look.

I don't think I've worn tennies since I was twelve. I didn't know what to buy, so I got a pair of Keds and some sturdier ones with a pink stripe down the side.

The truth is . . . I'm not exactly the outdoorsy type. I guess You know that. You're the One who made me this way. But seriously, this could turn out to be such a disaster! So I'm asking You to help me not do anything embarrassing or humiliating or ridiculous—and to fit into Justin's outdoor world so that he gives me a chance and falls madly in love with me before the retreat is over. Not too much to ask, right?

I guess I'll see You on the other side of the wilderness, Lord.

Looking forward,
Lucy

P.S. Any chance I could score a seat next to Justin for the ride to Snowball?

Chapter Three

MATT WOKE UP WITH REAL ANTICIPATION coursing through him. The Ozarks never failed to inspire him, and spending a few days at their feet, with a stream of great activities planned, was going to do him good.

When he'd first mentioned the trip to Lucy, her reaction was nothing short of underwhelming. Never mind that it took Justin Gerard to get her warmed up to the idea; at least she'd managed to get onboard, and he was determined that they were going to have fun.

A broad smile spread over his face as

Matt thought of Lucy out in the wilds of Buffalo National River, baiting a fishing line or reacting to wildlife along the hiking trail. She'd always been a girly girl, and she'd seen her outdoorsy shortcomings as a weakness—something that would keep her from finding the kind of man she'd always hoped to spend her life with. But Matt saw those challenges as something entirely different. They were just part of the overall picture that was Lucy.

Goofy and sweet, elegant yet somewhat unhinged, with crazy-wild auburn hair that she worked far too hard trying to tame and a smile that was all red lips and white teeth. She could light up an entire valley with that smile. In the years that he'd known her, Lucy had managed to cast a strange shadow over every other woman who crossed Matt's path, and it was an occurrence he'd never quite understood. She was a sort of standard he held other women against to determine if they were fit for him. So far, few of them survived the glare. But if he ever did find a woman with some of Lucy's more appealing qualities, he thought he'd probably spend the rest of his life chasing her.

When he rounded the corner of her street, Matt immediately noticed Lucy in front of her house, straddling the curb, with her thumb stuck out in hopes of a ride. The bags on the ground beside her were unfamiliar and drab.

"Where's Mr. Vuitton today?" he asked as he stepped out from behind the wheel.

"Hiding in the closet. I thought these seemed a little less pretentious. I borrowed them from Lanie."

"Lucy, you are not pretentious," he assured her.

"Thanks, Mattie. But I didn't want Justin to get that idea just because I have some killer luggage."

He paused for a moment and then shook his head. "Whatever," he sort of sang as he threw her bags into the car.

"How do I look?" she asked, throwing out her arms and shifting from one hip to the other while the breeze caught her reddish-brown curls and eased them back over her shoulders.

"Unpretentious, to start with."

"Score."

"And very cute. Now get in the car."

She tossed him one of her wide, toothy grins as she clicked the seatbelt into place. "Here we go."

"Yes, we do," Matt replied, dropping the gear into DRIVE and pulling away from the curb.

* * * * *

The first thing Lucy noticed when Matt's Mini Cooper pulled into the lot was Justin standing at the back of Alison's Buick with Wendy Marshall.

No, no, no, no, no.

"Wendy's going? I didn't see her name on the list."

"I guess so."

Wendy had been part of the group for nearly a year, and she was one of those girls who was so pretty that they make other women's self-esteem falter. She had the kind of sun-kissed skin that men probably wanted to touch; long, straight, and silky blond hair; perfect almond-shaped blue eyes; a turned-up little nose dotted with tiny freckles. Wendy reminded Lucy of a cartoon drawing, and she didn't want her anywhere near Justin

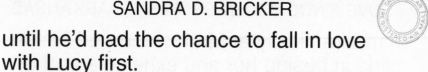

until he'd had the chance to fall in love with Lucy first.

She said a little prayer under her breath before hopping out of the car and meandering over to the Buick.

"Morning, everyone," she announced, and then she gifted Justin with the most dazzling smile she could muster.

"Good morning," he returned. Lucy noticed that his teeth were probably even whiter than hers. And she'd bleached hers the night before.

Matt loaded their luggage into the trunk of Tony's PT Cruiser while Alison wandered around with a clipboard, checking things off.

"I believe we're all here," Alison announced. "There are ten of us going and two cars scheduled to shuttle."

Before she had the chance to tell everyone which cars they were no doubt assigned to, Lucy took the bull by the horns. "So let's get this show on the road then, huh? Pile in!"

When Justin took her lead and crawled into the back seat of the PT Cruiser, Lucy followed him without pause. Rolling her hand frantically at Matt, she urged him to slide in beside her and exhaled a puff of relief when he did.

Lucy shot another one of her best smiles Justin's way and sighed again.

Thank You, Jesus.

Brenda took the front passenger seat, and Tony slid behind the wheel as the others made their way toward the Buick. Jeff and Wendy sat in the back with the new guy while Alison and Cyndi headed toward the front.

Lucy leaned forward and touched Brenda on the shoulder. "What's the new guy's name?" If anyone would know the 411, it would be Brenda.

"Rob Hogestyn," she replied, and she spun all the way around in her seat. "His family owns most of San Antonio's downtown real estate, and he's developing his own holdings here in Little Rock. He's already bought up a couple of key properties, and I hear he's going to build a condo complex just outside the Quapaw Quarter—"

And she's off!

Lucy glanced out the window and couldn't help but notice the disappointment on Alison's face as she glared down at her useless clipboard, her organizational plans undoubtedly dashed. Lucy felt a pang of guilt and resolved to let Alison arrange other less dire details during the retreat. Like who bunked where, which activities they would choose, and in what order. For the moment, however, the transportation seating was taken care of.

Lucy beamed at Justin. "Here we go!"

By the time they reached I-40 and headed west, Lucy had learned about Justin's upbringing in Charlotte, his aunt Sadie's recipe for chocolate peanut butter ice cream, and his longtime penchant for rare rib eye steak and roasted asparagus.

"Now that's the perfect meal," he told them. "Nothing beats it."

"I couldn't really say what the perfect meal is," Lucy chimed in. "It depends on my mood on any given day. I guess I just like variety. Some days, a glass of chocolate milk and a few Oreo cookies seem like the perfect meal."

Stop talking now, she warned herself. *Just stop talking.*

When they merged onto US-65 and turned north toward Harrison, Lucy decided to keep asking Justin questions so she couldn't make a fool of herself by talking too much. She pretended to be absolutely engrossed as he told her all about his work as a contractor and the perils of owning and operating one's own business.

This is actually going pretty well, she thought. *I wonder if I should ask him—*

"So what can you tell me about Wendy?"

A needle scratched its way entirely across the record of their conversation, and Lucy's brain thudded to a stop.

He finally talks about someone else, and it has to be Wendy?

"Wendy?"

"Yeah," he said. "She's really cute."

Digging her nails into the seat belt, Lucy swallowed around the sudden lump in her throat and plastered a smile across her face.

"She really is, isn't she?" she said, nodding.

Matt's elbow pressed into Lucy's

side, and she leaned against it in acknowledgment.

"But I don't know much more about her than that. We've never really had the opportunity to talk beyond the typical courtesies."

Brenda reeled around in her seat again and looked Justin square in the eye. "I know Wendy pretty well. She had dinner at my house a couple of weeks ago, and since we share an appreciation for George Clooney, we caught his latest movie at the Rave."

"How was that?" Lucy interrupted. "The reviews were pretty good."

"Oh, who knows. I don't care what he says or what his movies are about," Brenda cracked, and she broke out into a short fit of high-pitched laughter. "It's George Clooney, for crying out loud."

Lucy couldn't help herself. She turned to the left and looked Matt directly in the eyes. An entire wordless conversation passed between them before Lucy faced forward again.

"Anyhoo," Brenda sang, "Wendy Marshall. She's twenty-seven years old, and she's spent her entire life in Little Rock. Never lived anywhere else. She's a preschool teacher, graduated from the University of Arkansas."

"Sheesh, Bren. What was her grade point average?" Lucy cracked, and Brenda's expression betrayed no amusement whatsoever.

Matt laughed out loud, and Tony and Justin joined in. Finally, Brenda managed to break a smile.

"A preschool teacher," Justin commented. "That's admirable. Do you know if she's seeing anyone?"

"She was," Brenda replied. "But they split up about six months ago, and she hasn't been out with anyone since."

Matt slipped his hand into the crook of Lucy's arm and gave it a squeeze. She knew he was feeling her pain, and she appreciated his show of support. It didn't help, of course. But she appreciated it just the same.

By the time the group rolled into camp, Lucy could hardly wait to get out of the car. Her ego wasn't the only thing that had been bruised on the long ride from Little Rock to Snowball, and she groaned as she emerged from the back of the PT Cruiser, needing to stretch her stiff legs.

"Okay, boys and girls, listen up!" Alison called to them, clipboard in hand. She was almost glowing, and Lucy supposed she'd gotten over the disappointment of not orchestrating who would ride in which seat. It seemed she was going to make up for it now.

She's gotten her second organizational wind.

"We've got these first three cabins, and I've made up your room assignments. In Cabin A, Cyndi will occupy the bedroom with the double bed, and Lucy and Wendy will have the other bedroom with the two twins."

Lucy's heart sank. Sharing a room with her newfound competition seemed unfortunate and ironic.

"Brenda and I will take the studio, which is Cabin B. In Cabin C, there are two bedrooms with twin beds. Justin and Tony will take one of them, and Matt and Rob will take the other. Jeff, you can have the loft on account of your back troubles. There's a firm mattress on the bed up there."

"Thanks, Alison."

"Now let's take an hour or so to get settled," she told them as she tapped the face of her watch.

A tour guide on too much caffeine, Lucy thought.

"Have a look at these," Alison instructed, passing a sheet of paper to each of them. "This is our daily activity schedule. If you have any questions, just let me know."

"Don't be late for the bus. Because we *will* leave without you," Tony said softly, and Lucy snickered in spite of her best effort not to.

Matt had already begun unloading the luggage from the back of the PT Cruiser, and Lucy saw her opportunity to speak to him alone.

"Mattie," she whispered as he handed off her bag, "you have to help me out and keep Wendy occupied."

He stopped what he was doing long enough to grimace at her. "What do you mean? How am I supposed to do that?"

"I don't care how you do it. Just keep her away from Justin so I have a chance."

Matt groaned and shook his head as

he lifted his own bag from the cargo trunk and planted it on the ground with a *thump.*

"What are you two whispering about?" Alison asked as she stepped between them.

"You're doing a great job keeping us organized, Ali," Matt told her. "Nice work. Keep it up."

Lucy knew he'd encouraged the behavior as a direct hit to her, but Alison beamed like a neon sign in Las Vegas. "Thank you, Matthew. Really. Thank you for noticing."

Without a glance in Lucy's direction, he grabbed his bag and headed off toward Cabin C.

"Ready, roomie?" Wendy said with a smile, and Lucy tried her hardest to return it.

"Ready!"

"Let's all meet up at the lodge for an early lunch," Alison called after them. "Right down there, everyone. At eleven thirty. After that, we're off to the river to fish for our dinners!"

When they made it to Cabin A, Lucy followed Wendy into the bedroom and plunked down on the bed farthest from the door. She dragged her bags up beside her on the mattress and reached down into the side pocket of the backpack, producing a snack pack of Oreo cookies that she immediately opened.

Munching on one of them in silence, Lucy looked around the bedroom at the charming patchwork quilts covering each bed and the understated country ambiance. A border painted the same pale yellow as the rest of the room created the look of a floral pattern engraved right into the walls. The subtle and distinct touches, such as a single Gerbera daisy tucked into a small lavender vase and a handcrafted ribbon bookmark peeking from the pages of the Bible on the mission-style dresser, made the room come alive with personality. Despite the obvious differences, she was reminded of the Conroy. Hers was a five-star boutique hotel in the heart of the city, but this little campsite of log cabins and picnic tables in Snowball, Arkansas, was a five-star retreat.

Lucy watched Wendy pull back her

golden hair and twist it around her hand into a knot at the back of her head. The clothes inside her suitcase were folded into perfect squares and stacked like neat little crackers in a box. She pulled a pair of sneakers from the inside pocket, and Lucy's jaw clenched. They were a slightly-worn spitting image of her new tennies with the pink stripe down the sides.

She takes everything!

"I'll take the top two drawers, and you can have the bottom two?" she asked, and Lucy nodded as she crunched.

Taking the best drawers, too, huh?

"And there are only about six hangers in the closet. Okay if we split them?"

"Mmm-hmm," Lucy acknowledged.

"Oooh, those look good," Wendy said with a smile so bright that it could have caused a glare.

"You want one?"

"Could I?"

Lucy held out the package to her, and Wendy took one of the cookies and plopped down on her bed to enjoy it.

"Oreos are the best, aren't they?"

"There is no better cookie," Lucy

agreed, slipping one shoulder up in a halfhearted shrug.

"I know it makes me a big nerd, but I also like Fig Newtons."

"That's Mattie's favorite cookie."

"Really?" Wendy asked, looking for all the world as if she were really interested. "They're so great. I could easily put away half a package of them in one sitting if I'm not careful."

All right now. Stop being my cookie kindred spirit. I need to not like you!

"Do you want some help unpacking?" Wendy asked with a sweetness that made Lucy pop another cookie into her mouth.

"Uh-uh," she replied, and then she swallowed. "Thanks, though."

Wendy scooted back on the bed and leaned against the wall while Lucy unpacked.

"I wonder what's for lunch," Wendy mused.

"Whatever it is, I'm sure Alison has it all color-coded and arranged to coordinate with our place cards."

Wendy laughed out loud at that. "She

could be the most organized person I've ever met in my entire life."

"Ya think?" Lucy asked her with an arched brow, and they both chuckled, despite Lucy's best effort against it.

It was going to be much harder to dislike this woman than Lucy could have anticipated. In fact, to make matters just about as bad as they could be, she felt like they could actually make a pretty good pair of friends. And that thought just about ruined her whole day.

* * * * *

The lodge was small but charming. Cobalt blue vases held pale chrysanthemums at the center of every redwood table and bench in the place. A floor-to-ceiling hedge of glass at the back allowed a spectacular view of breathtaking and colorful scenery, contrasting the homespun quilts and intricate, wood-framed leaf fossils displayed on the opposite wall.

When Lucy noticed Alison setting out name cards on the long table by the window, she immediately turned to Wendy and the two of them burst into laughter.

"What's so funny?" Matt asked her, but Lucy just shook her head and slipped her arm into his.

"What's for lunch?" she asked him.

"They're setting out a buffet for everyone in about ten minutes."

Other visitors began meandering in just then, filling the rest of the tables. The delicate *pop-pop-pop* of a ping-pong game started on one side of the high-ceilinged room, and several dart games ensued along the line of half a dozen wood-shuttered boards.

"Listen, Mattie," Lucy said as she covertly changed the name cards on their table to seat Matt next to her and Justin across from them rather than at the end of the table next to Wendy. "Please don't be mad at me."

"Why not?"

"Because you know I mean well?"

"No, you don't, Lucy. You mean for things to *go* well, for *you*. And that's just not like you."

Lucy sat down beside him and touched his arm. "Matt."

"You're interested in Justin. That's fine. You want to do things you hate doing just so you can fit in and impress him. That's your prerogative. But manipulating people and moving them around to suit your own interests, and your interests alone . . . well, that's something altogether different."

Lucy considered Matt's point of view, and a sharp pang of guilt pinched at the top of her ribs, just beneath her heart.

"I get it," she told him. "And I'm sorry."

"Good. Enough said."

"Do I have to put your place card back by Alison's?"

"Let's not go crazy or anything," he teased, and Lucy leaned over and patted the top of his hand.

"Lunch is served, everyone!"

Alison's announcement punctuated the line already forming at the banquet table. Lucy filled her plate with pasta salad and sliced fruit and made a sandwich on sourdough bread with turkey and Swiss cheese.

She made it back to the table before Matt, and she smiled at Justin as he scraped back the chair across from her.

"That Alison sure is on the ball," he said to her in a half whisper.

"What do you mean?"

"I got here early and moved my name card down next to Wendy's. She must have seen it and moved me right back here!"

Why does Wendy Marshall have to be so perfect, Lord?

Justin looked like a lovesick schoolboy when he asked Brenda about her, and he went to the trouble of moving the place cards so that she'd be seated near him. He obviously has his eye on her. And now that I think of it, he seems to be after her in all the same ways that I'm after him. What is this, high school? Maybe I should pass him a note in study hall or have Mattie ask him if he likes me.

I'm going to try to get my insecurities more under control this afternoon. She's just so beautiful and sweet and funny. Honestly, Justin would be lucky to have her. But can't he please settle for having me instead?

Something in my gut tells me to just kick back and see how You work it all out. I know I've said I'm going to try to do more of that, Lord, and I really am. Maybe after we get home from the retreat.

Eager and hopeful,
Lucy

Chapter Four

Lucy grabbed a bottle of cold water and carried it out the back door of the cabin to the wooden deck. Folding one leg underneath her, she curled into the corner of the rattan loveseat hanging like a bucket from the beams overhead.

The multicolored forest drooped over the slope of the hills like a flowing carpet, and the dazzling autumn colors took on the sparkle of loose coins spilled over the landscape. The sky stretched taut and smooth into a splendid canopy, so blue that it made her heart ache a bit.

Orange, red, and gold trees rustled in

the brisk breeze, humming a tune with their turning leaves, and Lucy closed her eyes and sighed. She imagined the fun such a creative God must have had in putting it all together. She liked to picture Him there, in the midst of a galaxy of nothingness, suddenly inspired into a frenzied burst of inventive originality . . . thinking up shapes and images, experimenting with colors, forming meadows with the palms of His hands, and using His enormous godly fingers to push mountains into being. This day and this scenery reminded her of how amazing and inventive her Father really was.

And I thought I was a design genius for creating a Tuscan-style wall in my kitchen with paint and faux stone.

"Are you ready to go?"

Lucy opened her eyes. Wendy was clutching her own bottle of water and was wrapped in a hunter green-sweater that matched the hue of their surroundings.

"Is it time?" she asked.

"They're meeting at the cars in about ten minutes."

"I'm ready," Lucy said. But would she ever really be ready for fishing?

Wendy perched on the wooden railing and smiled. "You look sleepy. Were you trying to get a nap?"

"No," Lucy told her. "I seldom sleep well when I'm away from home."

"The heart of a homebody," Wendy said with a grin. "Me, I'm the original wanderer. I can fall asleep anywhere."

Lucy took a long draw from the bottle of spring water and closed her eyes.

"I'm sorry. Am I interrupting your quiet time?" Wendy asked, and she hopped down from the railing.

"Not at all. I was just enjoying the scenery."

"Well, I think I'll leave you to it and go grab my bag. We're going fishing today! Won't that be fun? I haven't cast a line in a month of Sundays."

Her excitement brought a smile to Lucy's face, but as Wendy's tennis shoes scuffed across the deck, she wished she felt a fraction of the enthusiasm. All she could think about when she looked forward to the afternoon's activity were the worms that would suffer from the clumsy poke of a sharp, shiny hook.

Please don't let me look like a fool out

there, Lord, she prayed. *And it wouldn't hurt my feelings any if you arranged some private face time with Justin, either.*

She swallowed the last of the water from the bottle as she hurried into the cabin and headed for her room. After a quick glance in the mirror, Lucy took a deep breath. She'd bought this plaid flannel smock at Old Navy, and she liked the way it looked over jeans. This would be her chance to wear the new sunglasses with the burgundy frames, too.

Pay attention, Justin, she thought. *Just for you, I'll be the cutest chick in the hood. Oh, I mean, in the wood.*

* * * * *

Just a few minutes prior, Lucy had been awestruck by the scenery at Buffalo National River Park. But now her stomach came to a full boil as Rob handed her a fishing rod. She knew she must have looked like a lunatic when her eyes met Matt's, because he spontaneously snorted.

"Now remember," Alison announced, clipboard in hand. "The limit is two catches per person, and if you catch anything shorter than fourteen inches, you have to throw it back. We have worms over there by Tony or live minnow down here by Justin. When we get back to camp, Dave and Betty Sue are going to host a dinner on the lawn behind the lodge of whatever we catch, if it's not too cold."

Lucy looked around her to find Justin leaning over the pack of fishing equipment and helping Tony pull it out of an enormous canvas sack. The way the sun caught his hair made it seem like a halo. And when he laughed, Lucy's breath caught in her throat. He seemed so at home on the river, and she found herself wishing she'd embraced outdoor activities when she was younger and still had the chance. As it was, she felt a bit like one of those fish she was going to catch, removed from the river and trapped on dry land. Not at all like the girl Justin had described.

"He wants someone at home on a campground," Brenda had told her.

Not too into her looks or high-maintenance—someone who can cook a meal, she recalled, and Lucy inwardly groaned. She loved a great meal as much as the next person, but the only substantial meal she'd ever mastered in her own kitchen involved a salad, some spaghetti, and a jar of Ragu. And on at least one occasion, even that had ended up in flames.

Matt caught her attention with a quick, "Psst," and Lucy followed him down the bank. She groaned when he produced a couple of wiggling worms from the pocket of his khaki shorts.

"Remember what to do?"

"It's burned into my memory."

Matt chuckled as he attached the hook to the end of the line and held it steady.

"Go ahead."

Lucy looked up at him, biting the corner of her bottom lip until she thought it might bleed.

"What?"

"I can't feel my legs," she whispered.

One side of Matt's mouth quivered, and he quickly poked the worm with the hook and gave her a wink.

"Good job," he said out loud as Justin,

Wendy, and Brenda approached them. "Want to bait mine?"

"What are you, a girl?" Lucy cried, tossing her hair and rolling her eyes. "Bait it yourself."

She sent an unspoken thank-you Matt's way with an apologetic grin.

It seemed to Lucy that two minutes hadn't passed since Wendy had cast her line, and now she was wailing with excitement.

"I've got a bite! I've got a bite!"

Justin, Rob, and Tony were at her side at once, and it appeared to take all four of them to reel the thing in. Lucy muffled a scream when the fish took two consecutive acrobatic leaps right out of the river and then actually walked across the water's surface on its tail.

"He's a fighter," Justin called out, and the rest of the group moved in to watch and cheer them on.

When they finally reeled it in, Wendy was hopping up and down, high-fiving people as Justin dumped the captured fish into a large rectangular container. Before they closed the lid, Lucy noticed its beady red-gold eyes. It reminded her of a demonic shark she'd once seen in a late-night movie, and she had never quite broken free of the memory.

"I don't think we have to measure that one, Wen," Alison called to her. "It's well over the fourteen inches long."

"Smallmouth bass," Jeff commented to Lucy. "They fight hard, but they sure do taste good."

Lucy pushed a smile up to her face and then gagged back the wave of nausea that moved through her.

"Hold it together, girl," Matt whispered, and he rubbed her back between the shoulder blades.

"Did you see those eyes?"

"Fish eyes, Luce."

"Demon eyes," she corrected him with a shudder. "Blecch."

"They love to hang out in the weedy patches," Justin told them. He smiled at Lucy and added, "You should cast out in that direction."

She rummaged around for that smile again and pasted it on before reeling in her line and recasting, almost hoping there were no more red-eyed family members hanging out nearby.

Brenda had passed on the actual fishing, opting instead to paint her fingernails and watch the others from atop a nearby boulder. Wendy joined her there after bagging another whopper, and soon Matt and Justin followed suit. It seemed, in fact, as if everyone with a rod and reel in their hands had snagged themselves a respectable catch or two except for Lucy.

When she finally did get movement on her line, it turned out to be some unidentifiable miniature fish that seemed to laugh right in her face when Matt removed it from the hook and tossed it back to its home. Afterward, her baited hook just floated around in the water, humiliating her with its inactivity.

"It's getting chilly," Alison announced. "So what does everyone think? Shall we make our way back to camp a little early?"

"Let's wait a few more minutes," Justin suggested. And then, to make matters worse, he added, "Give Lucy a chance to catch something bigger than the bait on her hook."

Funny. Just hilarious.

Turning her back to them all, she tilted her head upward and silently prayed. "It doesn't have to be on steroids like Wendy's, Lord. But something?"

Ten minutes later, Lucy felt a tug on the line. Then another.

"Mat–tie."

By the time Matt reached her side, the line had extended out to its limit, and it was all she could do to hang on to the rod.

"It's huge, Mattie!" she cried. "I can't even hold it!"

As the others gathered around her, Lucy pumped the reel with one steady turn after another, biting down on her lip as she did. Her catch fought back, but she was determined.

Matt forged in front of her and lifted the line from the water, holding the flailing fish up toward her.

"Oh," Tony sort of groaned. "Nice effort, though."

"It sure is a little one, isn't it?" Brenda asked.

"I'm afraid you'll have to throw it back," Alison told her. "Sorry, hon."

Lucy's heart sank as everyone, including Justin, returned to what they'd been doing before the excitement.

"Wait a minute now," Matt interjected. "I don't know about that. Who has the tape measure?"

Tony tossed it to him with an expression just south of hopeful, and Matt pulled it out with one hand while holding the wiggly bass with the other.

"Fourteen inches!" he declared. "We have a winner."

Lucy's enthusiasm returned, but only for a moment. It seemed that she and Matt were the only ones who saw the beauty in the moment. Wendy, however, gave her a very supportive pat on the back before walking away.

"Okay," Alison declared. "Let's toss the little guy in with the rest and head back for supper."

* * * * *

Lucy was quiet on the ride back to camp. Not just because she'd now gained the reputation for snagging the Mickey Rooney of the Arkansas smallmouth bass

91

community, but because of the look in Mickey Rooney's eyes when she had.

She'd often thought that, if she didn't love chicken wings and cheeseburgers and New York strip so much, she'd probably be a vegetarian. Chickens weren't so adorable, of course. But big-eyed cows never failed to tug at her culinary heartstrings. Even so, she'd never once looked directly into the face of her dinner at the moment it was forced to give its life for her.

Lucy wasn't sure she would ever eat meat and fish in the same way again, and she felt oddly irritated with Justin Gerard for being at the heart of these horrible feelings. It was for him, after all, that she'd murdered two worms and a baby bass in just a few hours' time.

"What's up with you?" Matt asked her as they strolled up the hill toward the cabins.

"I can't get those eyes out of my head."

"The fish eyes?"

"Yes," she replied in defense. "Mattie, did you see the way it looked at me?"

When he didn't respond, she turned to find him suppressing a wayward smile.

"Matt!"

"I know. I'm sorry. I did wonder how you were going to take this."

"I think I need to be a vegetarian."

"You do know that means giving up burgers, right?"

"Well, I was thinking I could be a vegetarian with special circumstances."

A laugh popped out of Matt like a single cannon fire.

"I mean like never eating any living thing that I've looked in the face beforehand."

"Ah. So you'll still partake of the cows and the fish. You just don't want to know where they come from."

"Kinda."

"I think that might be a good idea."

"And no more chicken wings."

"Really."

"Well, they look so much like little chickens, Matt."

"Understandably. Because they are indeed the wings of small chickens, Luce."

Lucy stopped in her tracks, tugging at Matt's arm until he stood still and looked at her.

"Please don't make fun of me."

"I'm sorry."

"I feel kind of sick from today."

"I know."

"I don't think I can eat dinner, Mattie."

"There will be other things to eat."

"But you'll all be—" She paused and shuddered and then choked back a gag. "I don't think I can watch you people eat them."

"Go and get cleaned up. Then if you still feel that way, I'll make your excuses."

It was a good plan.

A few minutes later, Lucy was standing in the shower and letting the warm water cascade over her. The only trouble was, every time she closed her eyes, tiny golden-red marbles looked back at her.

Wrapped in a towel, she perched on the edge of her bed and ran a comb through her long hair, trying to think about anything other than flopping tails or wiggly worms.

"Today was such fun, wasn't it?" Wendy asked as she plopped down on her own bed. "I haven't had that much fun in ages."

Lucy just smiled and flicked on the blow dryer.

Nothing like a little noise to cut down on the conversation.

By the time Lucy had diffused her curls, Wendy had moved into the tiny bathroom to take her turn in the shower, and Lucy was free to get dressed and apply some makeup in peace. She was tying the laces on the shoes that matched Wendy's older pair when Wendy herself emerged.

She looked like a commercial for shower gel. Her silky blond tresses were wet and hanging loose around her shoulders. Her heart-shaped porcelain face was scrubbed clean and looked annoyingly perfect without a speck of makeup. And her long, shapely legs poked out from the folds of the terry-cloth robe as she moved across the room, completely unaware that she was mocking Lucy and making her feel wildly unfit for a secret competition for Justin's affections.

"Do you mind if I don't wait for you?" Lucy asked her. "I thought I'd make my way down to the lodge and have some tea."

"Not at all. I'll see you there in a little while."

Wendy was such a sweet person. A little pang of guilt tugged at Lucy's spirit for pitting herself against such an unwitting and kindhearted opponent. But the moment she stepped into the lodge, those thoughts melted away into featherweight petals, blown far away by the breeze of Justin's presence.

"Hey there," he greeted her, his warm smile stroking her cheeks and staining them pink.

"Hi."

"Don't you look fresh and pretty," he commented.

"Thank you."

Lucy realized it was sort of ridiculous how much she valued those few words spoken by him.

"Dinner's fired up outside, but it's a little colder out there than I'd anticipated, so I came in for some coffee. Can I get you some?"

"Is there tea?"

"Down at the end of the table."

She could feel his gaze on her as she lobbed a tea bag into a cup of hot water.

"The other folks here on retreat belong to a family reunion," he told her. "They went after trout up at White River. I think there will be quite a feast for all of us tonight."

"Oh." She tossed the used tea bag into a small bowl and doctored her cup with milk and sweetener. "How nice."

"You had some bad luck out there today," he commented.

"Well, it's like that some days, isn't it?"

"It sure is. I remember sitting in a rowboat with my buddy down in Grapevine Lake, near Dallas. He caught catfish and bass on one side of that boat, and I sat there all day without a single bite on the other side."

The warmth of his empathy soothed her nearly as much as the tea, and Lucy took a deep, slow breath before drinking a little more.

"Want to take a walk outside?" Justin asked her. Her heart began to pound relentlessly against the wall of her chest before rumbling up into her throat.

"Sure."

Several large barbecue grills were set up on the stone patio, and redwood picnic tables draped in blue gingham cloths dotted the lawn. Lucy and Justin meandered over toward one of the workstations where Betty Sue, the owner of the camp, was filling empty corn husks with bass filets and then sprinkling them with salt, pepper, and lemon juice. Lucy looked away.

"I've never seen that done before," Justin told Betty Sue, oblivious to Lucy's avoidance of the table. "Can I help?"

"Of course," she replied. "Go and wash your hands real good, and slip on some of the plastic gloves in the box by the sink."

"You'll be here when I get back?" he asked Lucy, and she nodded eagerly.

Justin hurried off to do as he'd been instructed, and Lucy looked up to catch Betty Sue's eye on her.

"There's going to be baked yams and macaroni salad, some steamed string beans, and a lovely butternut squash," the woman said, and she smiled at Lucy with a knowing glint in her eyes. "You'll find plenty to eat on the table over there without ever passing by the grills."

"It shows?"

"Only to the trained professional."

Lucy chuckled and then touched Betty Sue's arm. "Thank you."

"No problem, sugar."

Lucy held her ground as Betty Sue continued with the preparations. After a moment, she felt the presence of someone beside her and glanced over to find a small girl standing there.

"I'm Annie," the child said, her large green eyes glistening.

"Hi, Annie. I'm Lucy. You must be with the family reunion group."

"Yeah. That's us."

The two of them stood there, side by side, both of them folding their arms and staring straight ahead. Lucy realized suddenly that they must look like life-size and miniature versions of the same statue.

The little girl finally broke the silence. "We caught bunches of fishes today."

"I'm sorry to tell you, so did we."

"It was gross."

"It sure was."

"And now we gotta eat 'em," Annie said incredulously, and she turned and faced Lucy with a contorted face that made her want to laugh. "Can you believe that?"

"I can believe it. We're eating ours, too."

"I'm not gonna do it."

"I hear ya."

"I'm six, and I'm not gonna."

"I'm twenty-nine, and I don't think I will either."

Lucy and the little girl both tossed their curls over one shoulder and shook their heads.

"I hope there's cake," Annie commented as an afterthought.

"Now there's a food I can get behind," Lucy replied.

The little girl giggled. "Yeah. Cake is good."

"Cake is very good."

The retreat is going pretty well, all things considered. I did have a few nice minutes with Justin, but I can't really get a handle on whether he's interested or just friendly.

My name was drawn after dinner, so I'll be leading tonight's Campfire Worship. We can do pretty much anything from singing worship songs to a scripture study, and I came back to the cabin to read my Bible and try to find some inspiration. I think I'm just going to choose one of my favorite passages and read it. Since Your word never returns void, I think I can pretty much count on that being an encouragement to the others.

And since You've heard me sing, I'm guessing You're in agreement with the reading thing.

All fished out,
Lucy B.

Chapter Five

"I WAS SO MOVED BY OUR SURROUNDINGS THIS morning," Lucy told them. "The blue sky, the gorgeous colors on the trees—and I was reminded that our Father created every bit of it for His own glory and for our enrichment and inspiration."

The ten of them formed a circle around a roaring fire pit. Wendy was directly across from Lucy, and she held a steaming cup of coffee close to her face as she gazed intently at Lucy. When their eyes met, her lips tilted upward in a smile that lit the sapphire embers in her eyes.

"So I was drawn to this passage of

scripture," Lucy explained, and she paused to open her Bible to the center. "Psalm sixty-five, starting at verse five."

Several of them opened their own Bibles to follow along as she read.

"By awesome deeds in righteousness You will answer us, O God of our salvation, You who are the confidence of all the ends of the earth, and of the far-off seas; who established the mountains by His strength, being clothed with power; You who still the noise of the seas, the noise of their waves, and the tumult of the peoples.

"They also who dwell in the farthest parts are afraid of Your signs; You make the outgoings of the morning and evening rejoice. You visit the earth and water it, You greatly enrich it; the river of God is full of water; You provide their grain, for so You have prepared it. You water its ridges abundantly, You settle its furrows; You make it soft with showers, You bless its growth.

"You crown the year with Your goodness, and Your paths drip with abundance. They drop on the pastures of the wilderness, and the little hills rejoice on every side. The pastures are clothed with flocks; the valleys also are covered with grain. They shout for joy, they also sing."

"Beautiful," Alison commented, shaking her head.

"That's just how I felt when I saw the foggy mist moving over those hills this morning," Lucy told them. "Like I wanted to shout for joy and sing. Of course, I thought better of the singing part." They all laughed, and Lucy exchanged a knowing glance with Matt. "I didn't want to scare any of the wildlife."

"On behalf of the elk and the humans alike," Tony quipped, "I thank you."

A passionate exchange of appreciative observations about their surroundings ensued, and Lucy was so happy she'd chosen that particular verse and that exact topic for their group time. No one was left out, and everyone seemed excited to share something.

"I've always been a bit of an outdoorsman," Justin told them from the folding chair beside Lucy. "Even at nine or ten years old, I can remember thinking what a magnificent thing God had done in creating the universe. But today, out on the river with all of you, I was reminded about the tiny details He's so good at. The glint of red in the eye of a smallmouth bass, the fire of red and gold in the leaves, even the sparkle of the smooth stones in the riverbed. Like the scripture Lucy read, it made me feel very much like singing."

"Why don't we?" Cyndi suggested.

Tony produced his guitar and started to strum, and the others began joining hands. Lucy's heartbeat was tapping much faster than the beat of the song as Justin reached out to her, and she slipped her hand into his.

He leaned forward and tipped his face toward her, smiling. And then he rubbed her hand swiftly with his own and whispered, "You're freezing."

She honestly hadn't noticed.

"We love you, Lord," Tony sang, and the others joined in. "And we lift our voice to worship You . . ."

Tony was probably the best singer in the bunch, but none of them were what Lucy would call especially gifted. Still, those ten voices blending together around the crackling fire, with nothing more than Tony's guitar and the chirping insects to accompany them, sounded like sheer, harmonious magic.

When the singing drew to a slow and sweet conclusion, Lucy closed her eyes and soaked in the silence for several long moments. When she opened them again, she met a tearful glance from Wendy across the fire pit. Matt was next to Wendy, his eyes still closed, and Justin slipped an arm around Lucy's shoulder and pulled her close to him for a moment.

"The presence of God is in His creations," Rob commented. "In our surroundings, in each one of us, He is alive and present. Can you feel it?"

They murmured in agreement, and Lucy nodded emphatically.

"This is a special night," Justin said in a soft, low tone. "I'm so glad you're here."

When he slid his arm away from her, Lucy looked up at him. The firelight cast a warm, orange glow upon him, and he smiled.

"I'm glad I'm here, too," she replied.

From the other side of her, Brenda

tilted her head down and let it rest for a moment on Lucy's shoulder.

"What a beautiful night," she said on a sigh.

"Who wants s'mores?" Alison asked, and everyone chimed in to voice their agreement.

As packages of graham crackers and marshmallows broke open, Lucy looked around at the nine other people with her. She'd never tasted s'mores, or even sat around a campfire for that matter, but the ingredients seemed to make it a no-brainer.

"How do you do this?" she whispered to Brenda.

"You put the marshmallow on the stick, like this, and you hold it over the fire until it gets all melty."

Lucy took one of the sticks from Matt as he passed them out, popping a marshmallow over the pointed end.

"Who wants more insect repellant?" Alison asked, passing a bottle to Cyndi.

At just that moment, Lucy's marshmallow went up in sudden flames, and she let out a little shout.

"Here," Justin said, placing his hand

over hers and drawing the stick toward him.

With quick little puffs, he blew the fire out.

"It's all black," she declared, disappointed that her marshmallow was ruined.

"It doesn't matter."

He took Lucy's stick from her hand and balanced it across his knees. Then he produced two graham crackers and placed them on Lucy's open palms. He smiled at her as he dropped a large square of milk chocolate on one of them. Coaxing the hot marshmallow off the stick and overtop the chocolate, he then closed up the two crackers like a sandwich.

Lucy took one bite and grinned from ear to ear. She would love anything that involved chocolate, graham crackers, and ooey-gooey hot marshmallow, even if she did have to cook part of it at the end of a stick.

"Whoa!" she exclaimed through a completely full mouth, and she caught Matt's eye across the campfire. "This is really good!"

He nodded and then took a bite of his own cracker sandwich.

"Why are they called *s'mores*?" she asked Justin, and he laughed out loud.

"Do you want some more?"

"Yes, please!"

"That's why," he replied with a grin.

Lucy watched Justin closely as he poked a stick through two marshmallows and extended it over the flame. He was handsome in any light, but the glow of the firelight was particularly complimentary. His square jaw and chiseled features were highlighted by the shadows, and his green eyes were now a deep steel gray.

"Here," he told her. "Get the grahams."

She withdrew several from the package and laid them out on her open palms, just like he'd positioned them before. First the chocolate, then the sweet, melted marshmallows, and two more dream sandwiches were created.

"Whoever thought of this," she told Justin at first bite, "was a genius!"

"Yeah, he was."

"Or she."

"Okay. Or she."

Justin suddenly reached over and ran

his index finger across the side of Lucy's lips, coming away with a fingerprint full of chocolate and marshmallow.

"Oh," she laughed, rubbing her mouth with the side of her hand. "You just can't take me anywhere."

"It's true. You can't."

They both looked up to find Matt standing over them. "I'm heading up to the cabin," he added to Lucy. "Want me to walk you back?"

Lucy considered it and then looked at Justin for an instant. "No, I think I'll stay here a little longer."

"I'll walk her up in a little while," Justin assured him.

"Okay. Good night."

"Night, Mattie."

"Mind if I join you?" she heard Wendy ask Matt as he made his way up the sidewalk.

Perfect.

By the time they'd finished their s'mores, Justin and Lucy were alone on their side of the campfire. Rob, Cyndi and Jeff were on the other side, chattering about the activities planned for the next day.

"Oh, horseback riding," Justin commented. "I'm really looking forward to that. Do you enjoy horses?"

Lucy paused for a moment before she nodded. "They're beautiful animals."

"They are. I've been riding since I was a kid. You?"

She didn't want to lie, so she formed her words carefully. "I haven't been on a horse in years."

"It's like riding a bike."

"That's what I hear."

She'd been truthful. The one and only time she'd been in the saddle was when she was twelve. It had been a short ride, since the young mare had thrown her about twenty feet and galloped away with her laughing horse friends, leaving Lucy to hike back to the stable on foot.

"I'm sorry to tell you that my horse's name was M. C. Hammer," he confided and then started recreating the melody of one of the rapper's most famous songs.

"So I guess tomorrow is *Hammer Time* again," she suggested, and Justin hooted like an owl.

"Let me walk you up to your cabin."

Justin stood and bent his arm at the

elbow, offering it to Lucy. She smiled and accepted it with a nod.

"Are you warm enough?" he asked her. "Do you want my jacket?"

"No, I'm good. Thank you, though."

They walked in silence, the cold fog of their breath floating behind them like clouds of cotton candy.

"I guess I'll see you in the morning at breakfast," Justin said when they reached the cabin.

"I'll see you then."

Lucy was so sure he was going to kiss her that she waited, frozen with anticipation.

"Sleep well," he told her and then rubbed her shoulder and arm briskly with one hand before turning away. "Good night."

"You, too," she managed to reply. "I mean, good night."

Lucy watched Justin jog up the gravel trail before she let herself into the cabin. A single white beam of light shone from beneath the bedroom door, bright enough to lead her safely through the dark toward it.

Wendy was sprawled across the bed on her stomach, her feet locked into the scroll of the headboard, her nose buried in a book. She looked up and greeted Lucy with a smile.

"Hey."

"Hey," Lucy returned, closing the door behind her and crossing to her own bed. "What are you reading?"

Wendy held up the paperback novel and showed Lucy the cover. "I'm a sucker for Christian romance."

Lucy laughed out loud at that. "I'd never have guessed. Me, too."

"Really?"

"Oh, yeah, I'm voracious about it." Producing one of the plastic containers of Matt's trail mix, Lucy extended it toward Wendy. "Want some? Matt made it."

"Thanks. Want a diet soda?"

"You have some?"

Wendy's mouth slanted into a sideways grin, and she produced a can from a plastic bucket next to the bed.

"Betty Sue set me up."

"Love her," Lucy said on a giggle as she pulled the ring on the top of the soda can.

A soft knock at the bedroom door caused the conversation to fall silent.

"Can I come in?" Cyndi asked, peering through a small opening in the doorway.

"Sure," Wendy replied. "Come on in, Cyn."

Cyndi padded across the floor, holding her ruffled robe shut with one hand and hanging on to a cup of coffee with the other. She dropped to the bed beside Lucy. Tucking a wisp of her short brown hair behind one ear, she asked, "So what were you girls talking about?"

"Books. Soda. Betty Sue," Wendy replied.

"Trail mix?" Lucy offered.

"Is it Matt's?"

"Yep."

"Sure." Cyndi dipped out a small handful of the mix and folded her legs beneath her. "I love Betty Sue and Dave, don't you?"

"We were just saying that."

"They grew up together, you know," Cyndi told them. "She didn't realize she was in love with him until he joined the military, so she followed him there. They were stationed together and got married overseas."

"Are you kidding?" Wendy exclaimed. "That's a romance novel waiting to happen!"

Lucy chuckled. "One of the couples that visits the Conroy every couple of months is like that. They met on a train from Paris to Nice when they were just out of college, and by the time they reached their destination, they were in love."

"Hey, you work at the Conroy?" Wendy asked her.

"Lucy's the head of Guest Services."

"What a great place," Wendy replied. "I love that old stairway in the lobby."

Lucy beamed with the pride, feeling how a mother must feel when someone compliments her child. She looked at Wendy, with her eager, sparkling eyes and her knot of blond spun silk piled on top of her head, and she thoroughly regretted pitting herself against such a sweet and interesting woman.

Suddenly Wendy threw her hand over her mouth and stared, wide-eyed, at Lucy.

"What?"

"Oh, Lucy."

Cyndi hopped on the bandwagon and gasped. "Oh my goodness."

Lucy's insides flopped over once and then again. "What are you two looking at?"

"Did you use the bug spray?"

"No."

"None?"

"No. None. Why?"

Cyndi and Wendy exchanged glances and then Wendy produced a compact from the bag beside her bed and passed it over to Lucy.

"Have a look."

Small red dots, maybe a dozen of them, created a speckled pattern around her throat and across her chest.

"What is that?" she asked them, touching the dot under her chin with the tip of her finger.

"Looks like bug bites," Cyndi said. "Do they itch?"

Lucy scraped one of them with her fingernail and frowned.

"Yes."

"Uh-oh."

"Oh boy."

While holding the mirror, Lucy noticed a few more spots on the back of her hand. Pulling up the sleeve of her sweater, she inspected her forearm and found another dozen or more of them.

"There are so many of them. It looks like the measles," Cyndi told her. "Why didn't you use the bug spray?"

"It's October. I didn't think I needed any," Lucy moaned. "Don't mosquitoes die off when it's cold?"

"You're right," Wendy confirmed. "But we're in Arkansas, in the woods, and near water. There are bound to be lots of insects still around. Biting midges, for instance."

"Biting who?"

"Midges. They're little bugs that, I'm pretty sure, stick around through the fall. They're also called no-see-ums, because they sneak up on you and you don't see um."

Lucy shuddered. "Perfect. A sneak attack. What am I going to do?"

"I've got calamine," Cyndi exclaimed.

"Better get it," Wendy suggested. "Hey, can you take Benadryl?"

It's not enough that she's my primary competition for Justin's affections? Now I'm kinda falling for her, too.

Wendy and I could be best friends in other circumstances, Lord. How unfair is that?

Please take the red dots away?

Itching . . . but hopeful,
Lucy

P.S. Next time, maybe You could remind me about the need for insect repellant before the bugs start biting?

Chapter Six

LUCY STOOD BEFORE THE MIRROR GRIMACING and holding her robe in front of her in a stab at modesty. Her wet curls were twisted upward into a messy nest atop her head.

"Are you sure this isn't some rare and horrible forest-related disease?"

"It's not a disease," Wendy assured her, sponging calamine lotion onto each little red dot on Lucy's back. "These are bug bites."

"I still don't understand why you didn't use the bug spray last night," Cyndi declared from behind them. "There was a note on Alison's activity list. *Be sure to use bug spray.*"

Standing there, shaking her head that way, Cyndi reminded Lucy of an elementary school substitute teacher she'd once had.

"Why, Lucy?" the teacher had asked in that same I-told-you-so tone. "Why would you paint your art project that shade of chartreuse? Now you're just going to have to live with it."

"One thing's for sure," Cyndi told her in an obvious yet futile attempt to comfort her. "You'll know better tonight, right?"

Fortunately, most of the bright crimson blotches were peppered over Lucy's arms, legs, and torso. Only two of the little buggars had made it to her face, and Wendy assured her that they could cover those with makeup.

One of them, the bolder of the two, sat right in the center of Lucy's nose. The other protruded from the slope of her jaw line, tipping its hat to her and staking its claim to her face.

"These two look like massive hide-the-women-and-children zits," she commented, and Wendy tilted her head over Lucy's shoulder to inspect them in the mirror.

"I told you about eating all that chocolate, young lady," Wendy teased, dotting the tip of Lucy's nose with calamine lotion. "One too many s'mores for you last night."

"Do you really think you can cover them?"

"We'll cover them, don't worry. But for now, let's get dressed," Wendy said as she replaced the cap on the lotion bottle. "Horseback riding today!"

Oh, yippee.

Lucy thought about confiding the truth to Wendy, telling her that she didn't know anything more about horses than she had about fish, that she was in it for The Guy and not for the love of the great outdoors. But even in her own mind, the truth came off as shallow and deceitful. She could only imagine how it would sound when spoken.

Instead, she smiled and nodded, as though riding a horse was the most exciting activity she could dream up for the day.

"Stop that."

Lucy arched a brow at Wendy. "Pardon?"

"Don't scratch them."

She hadn't even realized she was doing it. When Wendy turned away to focus on pulling her clothes from the cedar dresser, Lucy snuck in a few more scrapes.

"Lucy." Wendy hadn't even turned around.

What, do you have eyes in the back of your head?

"Don't scratch them."

"I can't help it. They itch."

"Think about something else."

A very large horse trotted across her mind's eye, and Lucy fell backward onto the bed with a groan.

* * * * *

As Wendy tucked her foot into the stirrup and mounted a beautiful chestnut quarter horse, she gave Matt a warm smile that reminded him of their conversation the night before. He'd walked her back to her cabin, and they'd stood outside the door for half an hour, chatting. Neither of them seemed to want to say good night, in spite of the frostbite that was setting in.

"What do I do?"

Matt glanced at Lucy and then did a double take. Her hands, her neck, even her face . . . freckled in red dots.

"What happened to you?"

"Bugs."

"What do you mean? What bugs?"

"Around the campfire last night."

"Did you use the repellant?"

Lucy sighed. "I guess I thought I was repelling enough all on my own."

"Wrong much?" Matt asked as he broke into a grin.

"Lately? Yeah. Now, tell me what to do with the horse."

"Well, you start by riding it."

"Mattie."

She looked so desperate and deflated that he regretted joking with her. "Come on."

Matt led her toward a horse with striking brown-on-white tobiano markings.

"This one looks like a good fit for you," he told her. "The American Paint Horse is a friendly, easygoing mount."

"That's what I want," she replied eagerly. "Friendly. Very, very friendly."

"Stand here," he instructed her. "I'll hold

him steady. Take the reins in your left hand and place your left foot into the stirrup. Then just grab the saddle horn with your right hand and pull yourself up."

Lucy looked around to make sure no one was watching and gave Matt a worried glance.

"You can do it."

Most of Lucy's five-feet, nine-inch height came from her legs, but when she pulled herself up to the saddle and tried to toss one leg over, she just couldn't manage it. Instead of mounting, she just hung there on the side of the horse, one leg flailing, and the other bent up like a pretzel.

"Okay, come down," Matt told her, trying hard not to laugh as he helped her. "Let's try a box."

He dragged one of the wooden crates toward her and positioned it next to the horse.

"Try standing on this."

"Oh, good. That will be better," she said, her almond eyes brimming with hope.

Stepping up onto the box, she took the reins into her left hand one more time.

She looked over at Justin to make sure he wasn't watching, bit her lip, and gave Matt an expectant nod.

"Left foot in the stirrup," she whispered. "Right hand on the horn thingy. And then just—"

In one fell swoop, she pulled herself up, tossed her leg over the saddle, and followed it in a slow slide right down the other side of the horse.

Matt hurried around the horse and lifted Lucy to her feet in front of him. Placing his hands on her shoulders, he looked directly into her eyes. "Let's try one more time, with just a little less of a thrust."

He could see that she was struggling to pull it together, and he kept her eyes locked to his in an attempt to keep her from falling apart. "You can do this."

"Okay."

"One more time and you've got it."

She seemed to brace with determination. "One more time."

Matt followed her around the back of the horse and helped her up to the crate again.

"Sorry," she told the Paint in a soft

whisper and then gave him a pat. The horse seemed to nod in reply.

"Left foot in the stirrup," Matt told her, and she complied.

To his great relief, she made it up and over.

"Good," he told her. "Now ease down into the saddle and put your right foot in the other stirrup."

She plopped down, but then nearly went over again when she began searching for it.

"Wait!" Matt exclaimed as he jogged around the horse and grabbed Lucy's foot. He gently eased it into the stirrup and handed her the reins.

"Never let go of these," he said. "Use the reins and your legs to tell the horse where you want to go. If you want to go left, pull them that way. If you want to go right, pull them this way. And, very important, Luce—if you want to stop, you pull them toward you, like this."

He gave them a tug and looked at her hard to make sure she was listening. To prove it, she pulled them back and then gave him a nod.

"Good. Wait for me to saddle up, and then you can follow my lead."

Alison, Jeff, Wendy, Tony, and Justin were already heading across the ring and through the open gate toward the trail when Matt rode up next to Lucy.

"Ready?" he asked her, and she gave him a tentative bob.

Clicking his tongue twice, Matt urged his mahogany Morgan forward. Lucy copied the click and then rocked back and forth in the saddle, obviously disappointed when the Paint didn't move.

Matt nodded toward his leg and demonstratively nudged his heels into his horse's sides. Lucy imitated the move and let out a little squeal as the Paint began to walk.

"Slow and easy," Matt said, moving into position beside her on the trail. "There's no need for anything else. Just take it slow and easy."

Cyndi and Rob rode up behind them, and Cyndi was yelping with each step her horse took.

"Slow and easy," Lucy reassured her.

"Just hang on to the reins, and take the ride slow and easy."

"Slow and easy," Cyndi repeated, her face contorted into a dried apricot. "Okay."

Matt let out a chuckle and shook his head at Lucy. She was nothing if not adaptable.

"Hey, where's Brenda?" Lucy asked, looking around.

"She doesn't like horses," Cyndi replied, her tone still two octaves higher than her normal speaking voice. "She's waiting back at the stable."

Painting her nails, no doubt, Matt thought to himself, amused. There was certainly no pretending with Brenda. What you saw was what you got. She didn't appreciate fishing, so she didn't fish. She didn't like horses, so she didn't saddle up. Matt wished a little of that would rub off onto Lucy. She was working so hard to become the kind of woman Justin would find himself attracted to that she seemed to leave behind a little piece of who she was with every episode.

He looked over at her and watched as

she held both arms out in front of her as if they were cast in stone, clutching the reins for dear life, with the Paint in a choke hold between her knees.

At least no one could ever accuse her of avoiding new experiences, he thought, and just then she looked over at him, her eyes as round as quarters.

"Relax," he told her, chuckling. "Let your horse do all the work."

"Hey, Lucy!" Justin called out as he galloped back down the trail toward her. "Want to race?"

Lucy's amber, quarter-shaped eyes turned to large saucers, and Matt thought he saw every bit of color drain from her face.

"Up to the big tree with the knotted trunk and back again," Justin told her as he angled up beside her.

"Um, o—okay."

"No!" Matt exclaimed, forcing a smile when they all looked back at him. "I mean, you stay here with Cyndi in case she needs you. I'll race you, Justin."

Justin shrugged and grinned at Lucy. "You call it."

"Ready," Lucy roared. "Set. Go!"

"Hah!" Matt shouted, slapping the reins and prodding his Morgan with both legs.

Adrenaline pumping, hooves thundering, Matt couldn't help himself and let out a bellow of a laugh as he reached the tree and yanked the reins to turn around before Justin even arrived.

"Hah!" he yelled again, and the Morgan flew down the trail toward Lucy, Cyndi, and Rob.

Lucy waved her arms, and he could hear her high-pitched catcall as he galloped closer. It spurred him forward to know that she was cheering him on in a race against Justin, and Matt cracked the reins again to go even faster.

When she covered her face with both hands, bracing her entire body for a collision, Matt realized Lucy hadn't been cheering him on at all. She simply couldn't figure out how to convince the Paint to move out of the middle of the trail.

"Whoaaa," Matt called, pulling on the reins to slow down as Lucy bounced harder in the saddle of the uncooperative horse.

"Move, horsey. Move, move," he heard her pleading.

After he came to a stop beside her, and the others broke out into applause, Lucy opened one eye with caution.

"Oh, thank the Lord. I thought you were going to send me flying."

Justin joined them in the next second, and Lucy melted into a smile that warmed the great outdoors by several degrees.

"Nice job, Frazier," Justin congratulated him. "You're quite the equestrian. How long have you been riding?"

"Since I was a kid," Matt replied. "My sister Lanie roped me into taking lessons with her for several years."

"I forgot about that," Lucy commented. "Lanie won a bunch of riding awards, didn't she?"

"Yeah, she kept it up long after I moved on to baseball."

Alison called to them from the top of the trail. "Come on, you guys! You've got to see this."

Justin led the way, and the others followed him up the incline and past the knotted tree. Matt thought Alison looked so excited when they finally reached her that she might just burst into song.

"What is it?" Lucy asked her.

"Look. Down there."

They lined their horses along the bluff and looked over the side.

"Remember not to look down too fast," Matt quietly prompted Lucy. "You know how you get with heights."

Lucy held the mane of her horse with both hands and leaned forward with caution as Matt recalled the day he'd had the misfortune of being seated in front of her on the log ride at Magic Springs Amusement Park. The instant they had completed the climb to the top, Lucy had made the very bad decision to peer over the side and look down. To this day, Matt could tell anyone who asked exactly what Lucy had consumed for lunch earlier that fateful afternoon.

"What are they?" Cyndi asked as she gazed down the ridge.

"Elk," Rob replied.

"Oooh, elk," Lucy commented. "I read about them on the Internet before we came."

Matt glanced over at her curiously.

"Well, I did," she told him before continuing. "There used to be Eastern elk in this area, like a hundred years ago, but they grew extinct. So I guess in the nineteen eighties, they brought in some Rocky Mountain elk and released them in half a dozen places around here. Now they've reproduced and repopulated this whole area."

"They're magnificent," Alison said on a sigh. "Just look at them."

Matt pulled a digital camera from the pocket of his suede jacket and aimed it at the small herd of five elk.

"They look like they should be pulling a sleigh," Wendy said.

"If it gets any colder, they might need to," Rob added.

"Do you think we'll get snow while we're here?" Cyndi asked him.

"Oh, no, I don't think so," Alison replied. "It's too early in the season for snow."

"I'm not sure you can really gauge that," Matt chimed in. "It is pretty cold, and if the conditions were suddenly right—"

"No, no, we're not prepared for snow on this trip," Alison interrupted, as if she had the final word on an inconvenient weather change.

Matt chuckled at that, never taking his

eye from the lens of his camera. At the click of the final frame, one of the elk looked up and made direct eye contact with the photo. The instant it was taken, however, the entire herd took off into the woods below.

Matt viewed the photo with pride, and Wendy checked it out over his shoulder.

"Look at that," she commented. "Like he's posing for a portrait. Just beautiful."

Matt raised his camera and pointed it at Wendy. She leaned down and put her arms around the neck of the Appaloosa and gave a broad photo-worthy smile. Backlit by a halo of sunlight that reflected off her shoulder-length blond hair, she looked almost angelic.

"Pretty," he commented, showing her the viewer.

"Goofy grin," she said on a laugh and then shook her head.

"I like your goofy grin," he told her, and it occurred to him that he liked much more about Wendy Marshall than her halo and her smile.

The only thing worse than the way a person's legs feel after horseback riding for the first time is the way they feel the next morning.

Remember how sore I felt that time I decided I wanted Jennifer Aniston abs and worked my core muscles at the gym for two straight hours? This is worse. And remember when Mattie talked me into trying the rock wall? Well, combine the torture of the ab workout with the morning after the rock wall, and this is still worse.

How did the cowboys do it, Lord? Didn't they ride for days, across plains and valleys, through all kinds of weather, and from town to town to town? I just meandered down a trail, up a hill, and past a tree that looked oddly like the ones that threw apples at Dorothy in the Wizard of Oz, and I could hardly manage to walk from my bedroom to the deck this morning. Waiting for my coffee to brew was excruciating. Never mind the humiliation of wondering whether I should call out for help to get over the tub ledge after my shower. It took half a dozen tries to get my legs to cooperate with me. I sure hope the aspirin kicks in soon.

And what was up between Wendy and Matt yesterday? I really wanted him to keep her occupied so that Justin could focus on me instead of her. But it never dawned on me that he might actually fall for her. Is that what's happening? Is Mattie falling for perfect Wendy? Is there anyone on this retreat who won't want to date her or hang out with her before we head back to the city?

It annoyed me the way he was looking at her, and I'm not really sure why. He's the perfect guy, and she's the perfect girl. It seems only natural that the two of them would notice each other in such a small group. In fact, she's just about ideal for Matt. So what's wrong with me? Any kind of friend would be happy for them both.

Cyndi hosted worship last night by leading a Bible study on the book of James. It's really one of the most practical books in the Bible, I suppose. For each problem James writes about, he also provides Your solution to it. If you don't have faith, here's what you do. If you resist the devil, he will flee. If you want to live a life of faith, then pray and read the Word. It's cause and effect. And it's all so simple, to hear James tell it. But life doesn't feel quite so simple for me these days.

For one thing, I have this burning attraction to Justin and yet I feel irritated when Matt looks at another woman. Am I really so selfish that I don't want my best friend to find love, just in case it might mean I'm not the center of his life anymore?

Then there's the fact that I'm inexplicably drawn to an outdoorsman who spends his time fishing and riding horses, both of which make me want to run in the opposite direction as fast as my muscle-torn legs will carry me.

Speaking of which, horseback riding is a pain in the thighs, Lord. A big old massive pain in both thighs. Not to mention the back, the neck, the arms, and all twenty fingers and toes.

Feeling like I'm sixty,
Lucy

Chapter Seven

"WHAT ON EARTH HAPPENED TO YOU?" BRENDA asked. "You're walking like my aunt Rose."

"I'm so happy you're amused," Lucy said, her face contorting as she eased herself down into the chair opposite Brenda.

"Good," she replied on a residual chuckle, "because I am amused."

"Traitor."

"Well, at least the bug bites seem to be healing up nicely."

"The great outdoors is taking me down, Bren."

"I can see that."

Brenda smoothed her helmet of black hair with the palm of her hand and then inspected the wine-colored polish on her manicured nails.

"This is why I passed on the fishing poles and why I didn't haul my fanny up on one of those horses," she said, leaning across the table toward Lucy as if she were sharing a secret. "I'm older than most of you here, and I need to choose my battles in a way that keeps me fresh. My time for trying new things is best spent in front of a mirror in a Macy's dressing room or sampling appetizers on opening night at a new restaurant. Neither of those activities is going to leave me hunched over with that pained look on my face."

At the moment, with her entire body throbbing like an open heart on an operating table, Lucy saw the beauty in Brenda's plan.

"Besides," Brenda said, her voice suddenly dropping to a whisper, "I want Jeff to see me at my best. And my ideal angle is nowhere in sight when I'm climbing up on a horse or standing in a river with water up to my knees."

Lucy snagged Brenda's gaze and held it there. "Jeff? Really?"

"From the top of my head to the tips of my toes, Lucy."

Jeff.

Lucy never would have guessed. She followed Brenda's eyes over to the buffet table where Jeff was doctoring a cup of coffee. The navy blue sweater he wore over khaki pants brought out the blue of his eyes, and his thick silver hair was cropped short around his ears and collar. Lucy couldn't hear the conversation, but when he shared a laugh with Tony, Brenda's hand rose to her heart and she came just short of an actual swoon.

"Music to my ears," she whispered.

"Brenda, I had no idea."

"Well, it's not like he's ever given me the slightest bit of encouragement, or even the time of day if I'm honest with you. But I keep hoping."

Brenda's entire face softened, and she looked to Lucy not like the oldest woman in the singles group, but like a schoolgirl in love.

"Please don't rat me out to him," Brenda asked her.

"I promise."

Lucy sent a prayer upward on Brenda's behalf. She would have reached across the table and squeezed her friend's hand afterward if not for the pulsating pain pounding through her body.

Matt and Justin came through the door of the lodge together, and Lucy groaned as she pushed herself up from her chair.

"I think you just made my aunt Rose's noise," Brenda teased.

"Laugh it up, my friend," Lucy said. "The first time Jeff Burnett invites you to ride a camel across the Sahara, my money is on the fact that you'll be walking like this for a month."

"Oh, you'd win that bet." Brenda chuckled. "But who are you out to impress? Certainly not Matt."

"No. Matt loves me just the way I am, thank the Lord. Unathletic, unadventurous, and completely unequestrian."

"Who then?"

Lucy paused for only an instant, making the immediate decision that enough secrets had been spilled for one morning.

"I have no good excuse, Bren," she replied. "Apparently, I'm just an ignorant glutton for punishment."

"Yeah, well, I think I'd give that up, if I were you."

Lucy's smile shattered as she took her first step away from the table and the burn of muscle pain sped through her body like a bullet on a mission.

What was I thinking? she wondered as she pushed her spine into a fully upright position and took a few more steps. *Why am I doing this to myself?*

"Good morning." She greeted Matt and Justin with a radiant smile that made it almost all the way to her eyes.

"Morning," Justin replied before he turned to focus on a cup of coffee.

"Why are you doing this to yourself?" Matt whispered as he leaned in close to her. "My nana had osteoporosis, and she stood taller than this."

"Hush."

"Go sit. I'll bring coffee."

"Bless you."

Lucy scraped the nearest chair away from its table and lowered herself to the seat with a thump.

"What's on the activity list for today?" Rob asked Alison. "I forgot my sheet up at the cabin."

"Oh, it's going to be great fun!" she exclaimed. "We're going on a three-mile hike out to a waterfall for a picnic."

Lucy felt as if she were falling, but before she hit the proverbial ground, Cyndi cried out on her behalf.

"Ali, I can hardly move from the horseback ride. The only hike I want to do today is from the buffet table to my chair."

I could kiss you, Cyndi.

"Why can't we do something a little less strenuous today and save the hike for tomorrow?"

The blotches that rose to Alison's face betrayed her. Appalled that the letter of the schedule was not being respected, she pursed her lips and sat down across from Lucy.

"Alison went to great pains to organize our daily activities," Lucy told them. "I work at a hotel. I know how painstaking it is to bring things together on a schedule."

Alison's features softened, and she looked at Lucy with gratitude.

"So if we want to change things around at all, I think we'd better give her a chance to look over the list and figure out which activities can feasibly be adjusted without unraveling all of the work she's done."

"Thank you, Lucy," Alison said with a rigid nod.

"Maybe we could ask Betty Sue about moving the cooking class to this afternoon. What do you think, Alison?"

Alison sniffed and pushed the wire-framed glasses up over the slight bump on her small, sharp nose. "That could work. I'll have a chat with her while you all have your breakfast."

Matt took the chair Alison vacated and slid one of two coffee mugs across the table toward Lucy.

"I suppose you'll be expecting a donation from me to your political campaign."

"Pardon?"

"Nice diplomacy with Alison. You could run for president with that party line."

"Oh. Well, she did work really hard putting all of this together."

"And I'm sure it had nothing to do with

the fact that Cyndi was your mouthpiece?"

"Not knowingly, she wasn't," Lucy said with a grin. "Can I help it if I'm not the only one all stiffened up like a starched shirt?"

"Well," he commented, "it did Ali a world of good for someone to acknowledge her efforts. So you do get points for that. Do you want me to bring you a plate?"

"No, I'd better go myself," she replied, pushing herself up from the chair with a suppressed groan. "If I stay too long in one place, you might have to get a shovel and dig me out."

Lucy spooned a generous helping of scrambled eggs onto her plate. Two biscuits with black raspberry jam and several spears of cold cantaloupe rounded out the fare, and she thudded down to her chair with a sigh of relief.

"What's that on your face?" Justin asked her as he joined the group and sat across from Lucy.

"Lucy provided a full meal for several thousand biting bugs out at the campfire the other night," Cyndi announced.

"Well, I like to be charitable that way."

"Yesterday, we thought she might have the measles."

"I'm sorry. I didn't even notice," Justin admitted. "Is it painful?"

"Not so much today," she replied. **In fact, I'd forgotten all about the bug bites in light of the excruciating pain in the rest of my body.**

"I think she looks kind of cute," Wendy offered.

"I see you're a little bit charitable, too," Matt interjected, and they all laughed.

"I do. They're like little red freckles."

"Okay, enough about my adorable gaping insect wounds," Lucy declared. "I incurred these battle scars in the name of my first experience with s'mores, so it was well worth the suffering. In fact, why don't we have s'mores on the breakfast buffet, huh?"

"Eggs and s'mores," Jeff commented. "I love good Southern cooking."

"Then you'll love your cooking class this afternoon," Betty Sue chimed in as she and Alison approached the table.

"It worked out then," Cyndi said. "That's great, Betty Sue. My sore thigh muscles thank you."

And mine as well, Lucy thought.

"Changing the schedule is just fine," Betty Sue told them as she tied the strings on a green apron with the State of Arkansas embroidered on the front.

"So what's on the menu?" Wendy asked her.

"You'll be broken down into teams of two, and Dave and I will walk you through all of the preparations for some beautiful Arkansas cooking," she said. "We'll start with sweet potato bisque and then put together a pork tenderloin with Arkansas Black apples and pumpkin jam, which will be served with a side of bowtie pasta with Cajun spinach and sweet onions."

The whole group moaned in harmonious anticipation.

"And for dessert, we'll create some luscious moon pies with graham crackers, fresh marshmallow cream, and dark chocolate drizzle."

"Hey!" Lucy exclaimed. "Gourmet s'mores!"

They erupted into laughter at that, and Brenda smacked Alison lightly on the shoulder.

"Now this is the kind of activity I can get behind."

"Unfortunately, it will also get behind *you*," Rob cracked.

"This is special-occasion dining," Betty Sue advised. "There are no extra calories when it's a special occasion."

"Maybe we could make it an extra special occasion then," Wendy said hopefully. "To make up for all the not-so-special ones."

"That sounds like a plan," Betty Sue replied. "I'll meet you all in the kitchen at three, and we'll bank on sitting down to a homemade feast at six sharp."

Lucy grinned at Matt with excitement. Cooking in a big group was going to be a barrel of fun, and best of all, it meant that the most exertion she'd have to put forth all day would be in chopping, mixing, or stirring.

When she noticed Alison seated at a nearby table making notes, Lucy was inspired with a stellar idea.

"Alison, can I talk to you for a minute?"

"Certainly."

"I wonder if you'd assist me in doing a good deed?"

"I'm always up for one of those."

Leaning in toward her, Lucy softened to a whisper. "When you're making up the teams, would you put Brenda and Jeff together?"

Alison arched a brow at Lucy. "Really?"

"It's supposed to be a secret, but I know I can count on you to keep it quiet. I just thought it would provide, you know, an opportunity."

"I had no idea."

"I know. Me neither."

"I'll be happy to assist the good cause of romance."

Lucy considered asking for one more leg-up in the romance department by pairing her with Justin, but she thought better of it. This would be Brenda's happy coincidence. Brenda was due.

* * * * *

Lucy & Matt — Sweet potato bisque
Tony & Rob — Pork tenderloin marinade
Jeff & Brenda — Pumpkin jam
Wendy & Justin — Spiced apples
**Alison & Cyndi — Cajun spinach with
   sweet onions**
Betty Sue & Dave — Dessert

Lucy quickly read down the list posted on the kitchen door. She was paired up with Matt. Unimaginative, but it was sure to be fun. Jeff and Brenda would be co-creators of pumpkin jam. Excellent.

As she read on, Lucy bit down on her lip so hard that she thought she might have drawn blood.

Wendy and Justin?

At just that moment, Alison stepped shoulder-to-shoulder with Lucy, shooting her a conspiratorial grin.

Yes, Jeff and Brenda. I see that. Nice work. But Wendy and Justin, Alison? Are you kidding me with this?

"Okay!" Alison shouted, clapping her hands together like the headmistress of a rigid prep school. "Let's pair up and man our workstations. Betty Sue and Dave will come around with further instructions."

Lucy braced herself in front of a pot of sweet potatoes and looked at Matt with an expression as steely as the stainless counter between them. His smirk told her that he understood her frustration, and when she picked up a knife with a six-inch blade, the fact that he immediately relieved her of it confirmed his comprehension.

"I can't believe—"

"I know," he empathized. "Just try to relax and have fun with your exceptional, albeit second choice, co-chef."

Lucy sighed. "I can't believe you said that."

"I just call 'em like I see 'em."

"You are not my second choice."

"No?" he asked her.

"Of course not. Wendy's my second choice."

"*Oh-hohoho*," he cackled and then picked up the knife for himself.

"And Rob was my third choice," she said, taking the knife from his hand and laying it to rest on the counter between them. "But you're a solid fourth, Mattie. And don't you forget it."

As the chefs started taking their places at the counter, Wendy stepped up next to Matt and smiled.

"We're spiced apples," she told him. "What are you?"

"We're sweet potato bisque."

Justin manned the station beside her,

and Lucy's lips quivered as she worked to hold back the smile from her face.

"Recipes are clearly written out," Betty Sue announced from in front of the sink at the end of the long counter. "They are laminated and placed at your stations, along with all of the ingredients. If you have any questions at all, just pull Dave or me aside."

"Ready, set, cook," Justin joked.

"Okay," Matt said, picking up their recipe card. "Step one says: 'In a large pot, soften the onion in the oil.'"

"I'll do that. What's next?"

"After the onions are soft, we add the sweet potatoes, beef broth, milk, and rosemary, and we bring that to a boil for a few minutes. Then we stir in the orange peel and juice and puree it in the food processor."

"Yippee," Lucy told Justin. "A kitchen appliance I've never worked with before."

"Is there a kitchen appliance you *have* worked with?" Matt asked her with a grin that faded the moment her eyes met his. "Sorry. Kidding."

"Let's start peeling the apples," Wendy suggested to Justin.

He picked up the peeler and started in on the dark red apple skins like a regular professional. Wendy looked at Lucy, and they exchanged wide-eyed surprise before both of them stared at Justin.

"What?" he asked.

"Where did you learn to do that?" Lucy asked with a laugh. "Are you a chef or something?"

"Oh, my mom was."

"Really?"

"Yeah. The pastry chef at a four-star in Charlotte."

"No kidding!" Lucy exclaimed, and she shot Matt an eager smile. "That's so great."

"My mom wasn't a pastry chef," Wendy remarked. "But she should have been. She loved to bake."

One more smile passed between Matt and Lucy before he picked up the pot and moved it to the stove top.

Sweet Potato Bisque (Betty Sue)

1 minced onion
1 tbsp. vegetable oil
4 cups cooked sweet potatoes
2 cups milk
2 cups beef broth
1 tsp. rosemary
¼ cup orange juice
1 tsp. grated orange peel
Black pepper and salt, to taste

In a large pot, soften the onion in the oil.
Add the sweet potatoes, milk, broth, and
rosemary and bring to a boil.
Simmer for 5–7 minutes then add
the orange juice and peel.
Puree soup in a food processor and add
black pepper and salt to taste.

Chapter Eight

BEYOND THE GLASS WINDOWS THAT WALLED one whole side of the lodge, the orange sun was setting beneath the cover of a lavender sky. As if to complement the sunset, Betty Sue had placed a deep purple chenille throw over the table on a diagonal. Ten places were set with unmatched china dishes, and lavender and sage votives glowed from a line of crystal holders down the center of the table, from one end all the way to the other.

Each of the teams was expected to serve its offering to the group, so Lucy and Matt were first up with their bisque. Matt spooned the soup into bowls, and Lucy carried them out to the table, two at a time, hoping all the way that she wouldn't trip or spill. Once the bowls were set in front of each member of the group, they all joined hands around the table and bowed their heads as Jeff led them in prayer.

After amens resounded all around, Lucy couldn't help looking from face to face, awaiting their reactions to the bisque.

"Oh!" Alison exclaimed. "This is so good."

"Fantastic."

"Mmm. Amazing."

"And it was pretty easy," Lucy announced. "I mean, I could probably make this by myself in my kitchen at home."

"That's the point we try to make with these classes," Betty Sue explained. "You don't have to go out to a fancy restaurant to eat healthy and delicious meals."

"I need to take you home with me for a week or two," Lucy teased, "just to get me over the rough spots of instant oatmeal and one-trick pasta."

"Hey, you could do a sort of revolving visiting chef thing," Wendy suggested. "A week with Lucy, a week with me, then on to Brenda's."

"But Brenda's a pretty great cook in her own right," Jeff told them. "Remember that lasagna she made last Christmas?"

"And wait until you get a load of the pumpkin jam Jeff and I put together for the tenderloin," Brenda added. "It's going to knock all of your socks off."

Alison gave Lucy a gentle kick under the table, and Lucy shot her an appreciative grin. They were seeing the beginning of something between Jeff and Brenda, and for the first time since they'd arrived, Justin had nothing to do with the fact that Lucy was really and truly thankful that she'd come along on this retreat. Despite the fish traumas and the bug bites and the horse-related body strains, Lucy was happy to spend time with this group of unique and extraordinary people.

"I'm so glad we came, Mattie," she

whispered, and he looked back at her as if she'd just said something surprising. "What? I'm having a great time. Aren't you?"

"Yes. I am."

* * * * *

It was at this precise moment that Matt identified the difference he'd noticed in Lucy lately. He'd been attributing it solely to her interest in Justin, but the truth of the matter ran much deeper than some guy who was half lumberjack and half underwear model. Lucy had been working so hard to become someone that she wasn't, with the fishing and the horseback riding and the outdoor activities, that she'd lost sight of the person she actually was.

Matt supposed that, like many people, his friend thrived when she was learning and growing. In the kitchen with the sweet potato bisque, she'd been trying with all her might to master something new, something she was actually interested in. Poking worms with metal hooks, however, and balancing atop large animals—those were not the things Lucy Binoche was made of.

Her joy was lighting up the entire room just then, fueled simply by the reactions of the group to the success of the bisque. And that glow was a shining beacon of a reminder that Lucy was not going to be happy, or feel satisfied, or even get what she wanted, by pretending to be someone she was not. How he was going to get this point across to his friend, he hadn't a clue.

Tony and Rob drew a roar of laughter by working together to carry a platter of pork tenderloin to the table that could easily have been maneuvered by one of them. As he looked on, Matt wished that his revelation would somehow make its way across the table, over Wendy and Justin's dish of spiced apples, around the pumpkin jam that made Brenda and Jeff so very proud, and directly into Lucy's spirit.

Somehow, though, the way she was smiling at Justin Gerard made him think there was very little chance of that happening.

But Matt knew a God who was bigger than his feeble wishes, so his heart sent up a fervent prayer that Lucy would realize there wasn't a man on earth worth changing for. She was really quite perfect just the way she was, even with an aversion to almost all things al fresco and a severe lack of personal balance. Her only real fault was a disturbing inability to see herself for the extraordinary woman she was. If she wasn't his best childhood friend, as much a sister to him as Lanie, in fact, Matt might swoop in on her for himself. But at the very least, he could pray for her, in hopes that she might find someone who could appreciate how special and unique she actually was.

Matt watched Lucy consume two servings of dessert, and he laughed when Betty Sue offered a third. She shook her head emphatically, which Matt recognized as Lucy-speak for regretting the second helping.

* * * * *

"Matt, do you want to play a game of darts with us?" Wendy asked, interrupting his thoughts.

He looked up into her smiling face and grinned back. "Sounds like fun. Though I should warn you, I'm not very good."

Matt followed Wendy to the other side

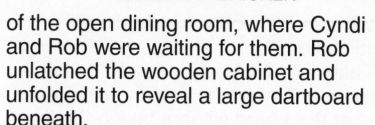

of the open dining room, where Cyndi
and Rob were waiting for them. Rob
unlatched the wooden cabinet and
unfolded it to reveal a large dartboard
beneath.

"Matt and me against you and Rob,"
Wendy said to Cyndi.

"Okay. How do you play?"

Rob picked up a large stick of purple
chalk from the wooden ledge and wrote
R/C on the chalkboard on the left side of
the cabinet wall and *M/W* on the right.

"Each player has to stay behind the
throw line," Wendy explained, pointing out
the strip of yellow tape on the floor. "We
take turns, one player from each team.
And the goal is to throw the dart into the
board, getting it as close to the center
bull's-eye as possible."

"You've done this before," Matt said as
he stepped up beside Wendy.

"A time or two," she replied with a grin.

Wendy proved her love of the game
over the next hour not only with her
enviable skill but with her obvious
knowledge. She was animated and fun,
using words like "skunked," "hat trick,"
and "chucker."

"What in the world is a chucker?" Cyndi asked her.

"That's you," Wendy teased. "You're a chucker; a player who just chucks the darts at the board without taking the time to aim. Let me help you. Come stand here."

Matt looked on as Wendy took great pains to show Cyndi the correct way to take aim before throwing the dart, and on her third try, Cyndi's dart actually poked into the board.

"Inside the double rings of the board," Wendy explained, "is the island. Up to now, you've been off the island. Now you're on!"

Cyndi squealed at the news, and Wendy shot Matt a sweet smile in response. They beat Cyndi and Rob two straight games, and Matt knew he had very little to do with it.

By the time they made their way back to the dining tables, Lucy and Alison had teamed up against Brenda and Jeff in a ping-pong game at the far end of the lodge. Wendy grabbed a couple of bottles of water out of the ice bucket on the buffet table and handed one of them to Matt.

"That was fun," she told him as they sat down.

"You're a dart genius," Matt remarked. "I just know how to throw them at the board."

"My grandpop taught me. He had amazing skill. And he used to build his own boards."

"Really?"

"Oh yeah. He was a woodworker, and he would carve these gorgeous, intricate cabinets to mount them in."

"So you've had more than a little practice," Matt realized. "I don't feel quite as bad about my score then."

"You have nothing to be ashamed of. Rob and Cyndi, on the other hand—"

They both laughed, and Matt chugged down some of the cold water.

"What's so funny?" Justin asked as he joined them.

"Wendy's a dart shark," Matt replied. "She looks like a nice, sweet, churchgoing single, but the truth is she's a shark."

"Shhhh, don't tell my secret. I was going to challenge Justin to a game later."

"I'm thinking there are not too many

things you're *not* good at," Justin told her. "From what I've seen this week, you're a regular sportswoman."

"A tomboy at heart, I'm afraid."

"Ah, the perfect woman."

Matt glanced across the room at Lucy, who was holding the paddle as if it were on fire and jumping out of the way of the ball rather than hitting it. She was different from Wendy in every possible way. The Anti-Wendy. Watching Lucy made him want to laugh out loud.

"Do you want to come, Matt?"

He'd lost track of their conversation in favor of his own thoughts. "I'm sorry. What?"

"We're going to walk up to the cabins so I can get my Bible," Wendy explained. "I think we're having devotions indoors tonight before the hayride."

"Oh, no. Go ahead. I'll see you back here later."

Matt saw Lucy's head turn as she watched Wendy and Justin walk out the door into the night. She snapped her neck back and glared at Matt. Klunking the paddle down on the table, she stomped toward him, swinging her arms feverishly as she did.

"Mattie."

"Lucy?"

"What was that?" she asked, nodding toward the door.

"A door closing?"

"A door closing," she said on a whisper, "after Wendy and Justin walked through it together."

"They'll be right back. They're just getting Wendy's Bible so she can—"

"But they left *together*," she pointed out.

"Yes. They did."

"Oh, Mattie, I don't want them going places together. *Alone*. I thought you were going to help me out with this."

Matt leaned against the metal chair back and regarded Lucy in silence. So much for his revelation reaching her spirit and all that. He could almost hear the rubber bounce of his prayer hitting the wall and ricocheting to the ground.

"Matt, are you listening to me?"

"Yes, Lucy. I'm listening."

"Well?"

"Well, what?"

She looked like Lanie used to look at eight years old when she didn't get her way, with her hand on one hip, clomping her foot down on the floor.

"You know what I was just thinking about, Luce?"

She didn't answer for a moment, but finally she softened and folded down into the chair beside him. "What?"

"Remember that summer when you got it in your head that you wanted to have a whole farm full of pet butterflies?"

"Yeah."

"And you and Lanie went out every day and caught them with a net and a mayonnaise jar."

"And then we'd take them home to my house and let them fly around the screened-in porch."

"And you just couldn't figure out why they kept dying."

"I was so angry at you when you came over and opened the porch door and they all flew out," she said with a nostalgic grin. "Why did you do that anyway, Mattie?"

"Because no matter how much you want to, you can't make butterflies live on the porch, Lucy."

"I know that. Now."

"Do you?" he asked her.

"Well, of course I do. I'm not ten years old any more."

"No, you're not. So when are you going to stop catching butterflies and caging them on the porch? Why don't you just go stand out on the ridge and watch them fly? You never know what else you'll see while you're up there."

"Mattie, what in the world are you talking about?"

He thought about it for a moment and then replied, "I don't have the first clue."

Matt stood up and walked away from her without looking back. He wasn't entirely sure why, but his heart felt heavier than it had in a very long time. Oh, he knew his concerns for Lucy were providing a good chunk of the weight, but that wasn't all there was to it. There was something else. He couldn't put his finger right on it, but it was there.

* * * * *

A stone, circular fireplace stood from floor to ceiling in the corner of the dining room, with copper screens on both sides. Ten chairs had been placed in a semicircle in

171

front of it. Once they had retrieved cups of coffee, tea, or hot chocolate, the group members took their seats in front of the blazing fire.

"Our newest member, Justin, is going to take the lead with our devotional time tonight," Alison announced. "Justin, we're all so happy that you've joined our group, and especially that you've come along on this trip so that we can get to know you a little better."

"Thank you, Alison. I appreciate that," he replied. "I thought I'd start out by reading to you from the book of Romans. If you want to follow along, I'm in chapter fifteen, starting with verse four."

Several of them opened their Bibles, and Wendy slid hers toward Matt to share.

"'For whatever things were written before were written for our learning, that we through the patience and comfort of the Scriptures might have hope. Now may the God of patience and comfort grant you to be like-minded toward one another, according to Christ Jesus, that you may with one mind and one mouth glorify the God and Father of our Lord Jesus Christ.'"

Matt watched as Justin folded his Bible shut and ran his hand over the leather cover.

"I've been a believer since the twelfth grade," he told them. "But when I moved to Little Rock, I just couldn't seem to find a church home where I felt like I belonged. When I came to Grace Community, I was pretty much at the end of my rope. I'd made friends in the area, but none of them were believers. None of them were like-minded. And I've come to know that that's such an important issue. Sharing who you are with people who know the same God and rely on His grace in the same manner—well, there's really nothing so important. We can't walk this walk alone, can we? We need one another."

Matt glanced at Lucy. She was hanging on Justin's every word, and Matt wondered whether she was gripped by the message or simply charmed by the man.

"It's been with a very light heart that

I've fallen into fellowship with this group of people. And I want you to know how much you've all come to mean to me."

Conversation over the next hour ran the gamut from the sharing of scriptures to further sentiment about what the fellowship of the singles group at Grace Community Church had come to mean to its various members. Matt had to admit to himself that he shared the appreciation they spoke about.

George Sedgewick came to mind, and he thought about how many years the two of them had been friends. But there was still so much George didn't know about Matt's core beliefs and feelings and desires, because he just didn't have a spirit that could understand them.

Matt recalled a conversation he'd had with George just a year or so prior; his friend had referred to the Bible as a "history book" and to Jesus Christ as an "influential historic figure."

"Could we pray for someone?" Matt asked the group. "A friend of mine named George is heavy on my heart, and I'd like to pray for his salvation."

Matt's emotions were sitting right in the

middle of his throat, and he enjoyed a deep, cleansing sigh as Justin lifted George up in prayer.

And while Your spirit is moving throughout this room, Lord, forgive me for judging Lucy. If Justin Gerard is the man You've set aside for her, then let it come about naturally and bless their lives with love. But if he isn't, open Lucy's eyes to Your will and let her find the man who will appreciate all of the wonderful gifts that she already possesses.

Another deep sigh and Matt opened his eyes to find Lucy looking directly at him from the other side of the circle, her brown eyes misted with golden emotion. Placing her hand sweetly over her heart, she smiled at him, a pinched-lip smile that dug deep grooves into her shiny pink cheeks.

Justin led devotions tonight, and he spoke about the importance of surrounding yourself with like-minded people who share your faith and beliefs. I was so moved by that, Lord, and I felt more convicted than ever that this trip is all about showing him that I can fit into his world.

I never would have imagined that, after praying to You about finding a life partner, someone like Justin would walk right into Grace Community Church! And this attraction that I feel toward him is self-evident, isn't it? He just can't be a coincidence meant for some other woman. I have to believe You sent him for me.

I know I don't share all of his hobbies, but I learned to make a sweet potato bisque by following a recipe, didn't I? I know I can learn to appreciate the things he likes in life so that we can share them.

Please start making it all go right instead of so horribly, horribly wrong. It seems like every time I try to impress him by doing something he loves, I end up making a fool of myself or getting injured or eaten alive. I mean, if You sent him for me, let me bond with him by getting something right.

Tonight we'll have a hayride. That seems safe enough—aside from the potential for frostbite, of course. But tomorrow's activity for the day is a trip to Blanchard Springs Caverns. I'm trying not to always expect the worst, but you know my thing about closed-in spaces, right? Alison says there will be air in there and room to move around but will there be ENOUGH of it? I mean, You know I need my space to feel really comfortable, so if You wouldn't mind filling those caverns with some heavy breezes, I'd really appreciate it.

Your oxygen-loving daughter,
Lucy Binoche

Chapter Nine

"WE HAVE THE BENDER FAMILY WITH US tonight," Dave announced. "They're here for a reunion. And then we have the singles group from Grace Community Church in Little Rock. I think you've all met one another—am I right?"

They nodded to each other, and Lucy felt the sweep of their glances as the three teenage boys from the Bender clan eyed her. Annie, the red-haired little girl she'd met the night of the fish fry, pushed her way from behind two of the boys and squeezed out in front of them.

"Hi, Lucy," she called out to her, waving.

"Hi, Annie. Are you having fun?"

The child sheltered one side of her mouth with her hand and squinted her eyes as she shook her head. "Not really. How about you?"

"Kinda, yeah."

"We're going to load you all up in the back of these two wagons," Dave announced, "and take you on a horse-drawn hayride through sixteen acres of the prettiest land God ever made."

"It's not like we're gonna be able to see it," one of the boys grumbled, and the other two snickered in response.

"There are blankets on the hay bales, so feel free to wrap yourselves up and stay warm. It's a chilly Arkansas night. There's also a supply of snacks and thermoses of Betty Sue's world-famous warm apple cider. So let's load up!"

"Annie, now don't forget," her mother said, "I don't want you sitting in the hay because of your allergies. Mister Dave said you could sit up front with him."

Annie looked at Lucy and rolled her eyes.

Matt climbed aboard before Lucy, took hold of both of her hands, and pulled her up into the back of the wagon. While she found a comfy spot atop one of the bales, he remained there and helped some of the others up as well.

What a sweetheart he is, she thought as she watched him.

Alison, Brenda, and Jeff sat across from her, and they were soon joined by the young newlywed couple from the reunion.

"Hi, I'm Brad Reynolds," the groom announced to them. "This is my wife, Sharon." He indicated a petite blond, who smiled at them. When an older woman with an unusually black helmet of hair plopped down with a groan, he added, "And this is my mom, Esther."

Lucy introduced herself, and the other members of the group followed suit.

Justin, Wendy, Cyndi, and Matt piled into the wagon as well, and everyone settled in with blankets while Alison poured cups of cider and Wendy handed them out. Justin plopped down next to Lucy and poked her playfully with his elbow. Lucy's skin tingled in response, and she was reminded of a past summer encounter with a swarm of ladybugs.

"So how many Benders are here this week?" Lucy asked.

"Thirteen," Sharon replied, and she began to name all of the family members as she pointed them out.

"This is the first time we've all been together since before Annie was born," Esther explained. "We came from all corners of the country, too."

"It's Brad's birthday gift to his mother," Sharon said, obviously proud of her husband's thoughtfulness.

"I wanted us all together just one more time before I die," Esther declared somewhat gruffly, as if that day might be just around the corner.

Lucy thought that Esther looked to be in fine health but her surly disposition could use a little improvement.

"Annie, you sit down like a lady up there," Esther called out, and Annie groaned an indecipherable reply from the front seat of the wagon.

Sharon gasped just then, and they all turned to see what had inspired it.

"How many lights are there?" Annie asked Dave excitedly. "I'll bet there's a gazillion!"

The horse had pulled the wagon over the top of the hill and onto a path lit as far as the eye could see by a winding luminaria of candles set inside sand-filled bags.

"Oh, Dave," Alison called out toward him. "What a sight!"

Betty Sue waved to them from the driver's seat of the second wagon. "Isn't it somethin'?"

They all shouted back to her in agreement.

"Beautiful!"

"Amazing!"

"Really spectacular!"

The horizon domed over them, a huge deep blue cup with silver glitter sparkling inside it. A perfect slice of a quarter-moon curved overhead, helping the candles to light the way.

Lucy took a sip from the plastic cup of cider and let the tart cinnamon warmth coat her throat. The chatter of voices dissolved into complete and utter silence, just the *clomp-clomp-clomp* of horses' hooves setting a simple and gentle rhythm against the night.

Jeff unfolded another blanket and

wrapped it around Alison's left shoulder and Brenda's right, leaving himself sandwiched in the middle of them. When his eyes met Lucy's, he shot her a grin and shivered from the cold.

Lucy glanced over at Justin, who raised an eyebrow and held out a corner of his blanket. She smiled as she moved into it, pulling it snug around her.

A slight tickle up inside her nose caused Lucy's eyes to begin watering. The tickle lost no time in progressing to a full-on quiver, propelling Lucy into a fit of sneezes, one right after the other.

"Uh-oh," Matt said in a monotone voice.

"Wha–wha—" But Lucy couldn't complete the question before another line of sneezes forced their way out.

"What?" she was finally able to ask.

"Hay."

"Hey, what?"

"Hay, Luce. Remember when you came with me and Lanie to my Uncle Ridley's farm that summer?"

Several more sneezes delayed her reply.

"Oh no."

"What is it?" Wendy asked Matt.

"Lucy's allergic to hay," he replied.

"Just like our little Annie," Sharon told them.

"Then why are you on a hayride?" Justin asked directly, and then he seemed to soften as he brushed a lock of hair from her cheek.

"I for–for–" Another row of three sneezes.

"She forgot," Matt told them, and he got up and leaned over the side of the wagon toward Dave. "Would you mind stopping for a second?"

"Whoa!" Dave called, pulling back on the reins until the wagon slowed to a standstill. "What's up?"

"Lucy and I are going to walk back to the cabins. It's not too far, and she's having a pretty severe reaction to the hay."

"Oh, I'm sorry," Dave replied. "Do you think it would help if she came up here and sat next to me and Miss Annie? Getting her away from the bales might help."

"Yeah, Lucy. Come ride with us," Annie exclaimed.

"Actually, that might work," Matt said, standing up and taking Lucy's arm. "Come on. Let's get you up front, Luce."

Aaaa-choooooo. Ahaaahhhhh-shoo. Ah-ah-ah-chooooooo.

As Lucy hoisted one leg over the back of the bench seat, she glanced back at Justin. His head was tilted toward Wendy's, and they seemed to be deep in conversation. She doubted that he would even notice that she'd moved up front with Dave.

"Mattie," she wheezed. "Are you coming, too?"

"There's only room for us up here, little lady," Dave explained. "But we won't bite cha, will we, Miss Annie?"

"Nope."

Matt shook out a blanket and handed it to Lucy before sitting down again.

"Ready, Freddy?" Dave asked her, and Lucy gave a halfhearted nod. "Hah!" he exclaimed and snapped the reins. The two horses set out on their journey once again.

The itching and twitching spread out across her face, and Lucy rubbed her nose hard with the palm of her hand before another stream of sneezes crept upon her.

Hah-chhhhooooooo. Aaaaaa-shoo. Hah-choooooooo.

"God bless you, times three," Annie offered.

Dave produced a cotton handkerchief from the pocket of his jacket and handed it to Lucy.

"Thanks," she croaked and then used it to wipe her nose.

* * * * *

Matt knocked on the front door of Lucy's cabin and waited for someone to answer the door. When it finally creaked open, he was met by a red-blotched and swollen version of Lucy, who rasped out an unidentifiable greeting.

She had pulled her hair upward into a ponytail and secured it with a gathered elastic band, and she wore bright pink flannel pants, a purple pullover sweater, and unmatched cable knit socks. She left him standing in the doorway as she thumped away toward the camel-colored sofa and collapsed on it.

"I brought Benadryl," he announced, closing the door behind him before following Lucy to the couch. "Betty Sue says it will help you sleep and get you breathing normally again."

"Dat would be dice," she replied through a stuffed nose and a closed throat.

Matt chuckled. "I'll get water."

He returned with a bottle from the refrigerator and read the back of the package before tapping out one of the capsules and handing it to Lucy.

"Take one now and another in four hours if you're awake."

"Oh, Baddie, what is by problemb?"

He couldn't help himself, and he snorted out a laugh.

"You sound like Rudolph when he has to wear the thing on his nose to cover up the fact that it lights up. Remember that cartoon?"

"Shud up."

"I'm sorry. Need anything else?"

Lucy plucked several tissues out of the box on the table and began to blow. It sounded like bad television reception that suddenly went wild.

"Just whed we were all cozy, sharig a blanket . . . this! And then did you see the way he was lookig at Wendy, Baddie? He was pretty quick to forget that I'mb alive."

"Come here," Matt said, and he opened his arm toward her.

She stared at him, deadpan, and looked about as sad as he'd ever seen her.

"Come here," he repeated, shaking his arm at her.

When she plopped down beside him, he wrapped both arms around her and pulled her close.

"Relax, Luce. Can you do that for me?"

She shook her head. "Uh-uh."

"Yes, you can. Just try."

After a long moment of silence, he barely heard her. "K."

"Okay."

Matt stroked her hair a couple of times and then planted a kiss on the top of her head.

"Just let things unfold, Luce. You're going to make yourself crazy with this. And frankly, you're crazy enough already. I'm not sure there's room for more crazy."

She laughed and grabbed for a tissue to dab at her nose.

"Hi, Matt," Wendy said as she came

through the front door. "How's our patient?"

"On the mend."

"I'm goig to bed," Lucy announced, and she groaned as she pushed her way to her feet and walked away from them. "Night."

"Good night," Wendy returned, and she smiled at Matt.

Once the bedroom door closed behind Lucy, Wendy sat down opposite Matt on the couch. "Quite a day, huh?"

"It was fun," he replied. "But I can't help thinking that maybe Alison over-scheduled us."

"I feel that way, too. It seems like we're doing something or going somewhere every minute of every day."

"I congratulate Alison on bringing this all together," he said with sincerity. "She worked really hard in putting every cent we raised throughout the year to spectacular use."

"Yes, she did. But a little reflective time built into the schedule would have been nice, too."

"I have to agree."

"Maybe we could wait until we get back and then suggest it for next time."

"I think that's a great idea."

Wendy's grin was brimming with mischief. "I'm full of great ideas, you know."

"And modesty. Don't forget that."

Wendy let out a hearty laugh. "Well, let me tell you about one of the really great ideas I've been kicking around. Then I'll give you some time to ponder it, and you can come back and tell me how brilliant I am."

Matt tilted his head and gave Wendy a tentative smile. "Why do I get the feeling you're going to zing me right now?"

"I'm not going to zing you," she told him, and there was a vulnerable lilt to it that took him off guard. "But I think I'm going to surprise you."

"I don't surprise easily. But give it a try."

"Okay. I've been thinking that maybe—"

Her words were broken in half as the front door flung open and Cyndi, Rob, and Justin filled the living room like a suddenly overturned cistern of wine.

"It is so cold out there!" Cyndi exclaimed. "I wish I'd known it would get this cold. I would have packed warmer clothes."

"What are you two doing here?" Matt asked the guys.

"We're gentlemen, Frazier," Justin teased. "We walked the lady to her door."

"Color me astonished," Matt said to Cyndi. "I didn't know they had it in them."

"Let's get out of here and let these women get to sleep."

Matt turned toward Wendy with a questioning raise of one eyebrow.

"No, it's fine. Go. We'll talk tomorrow."

"You sure?"

"Absolutely."

Matt rose from the couch and joined Justin and Rob at the door. "And here I was looking forward to being surprised."

"Well, I have a few of them left in me," Wendy said on a chuckle. "I'll save something for tomorrow."

"I'll keep that in mind."

Good-nights made the rounds, and the clank of the dead bolt punctuated their departure.

"What did we interrupt with you and Wendy?" Justin asked as they headed up the hill toward their cabin, the crunch of gravel underfoot keeping time to their matching strides.

"We were just talking about how over-scheduled we've been on this trip."

"What do you mean?" Rob asked.

"Something planned all day, every day. No downtime whatsoever."

"That's the way I like it," Rob said. "I can be a couch potato in Little Rock."

"Right, but this is a spiritual retreat. I'd just like a little more time to be spiritual."

"That's what nightly devotions are about," Justin interjected.

"Yeah, I guess."

"What's the matter, Frazier? Getting a little too old for all this action?"

"Uh, you're older than both of us, Justin," Rob pointed out.

"But I'm in better shape," he countered.

"Not to mention prettier," Matt said with a shrug. "Let's not forget what a pretty man Justin is."

Rob burst into cackling laughter at that, and so did Matt and Justin.

"I won't forget that, Frazier."

"Oh, don't worry your pretty little head, Gerard."

Justin landed a firm punch right at the center of Matt's bicep, and their laughter echoed out over the moonlit landscape.

Hay??

A beautiful moon, a romantic hayride through the hills with Justin right there next to me, and I'm allergic to HAY?!

Oh, Lord. What next?

I just realized what's next. Underground caverns.

I had to ask.

L.

Chapter Ten

THE FLOOR WAS SO COLD BENEATH LUCY'S bare feet that she took off at a full run toward the carpeted part of the living room. Wishing she'd thought to put on slippers, she rubbed her feet into the thick pile before crossing the next portion of uncovered hardwood.

Standing on her tiptoes, she creaked open the door to Cyndi's bedroom and stepped inside. When her eyes began to adjust to the dark, she crossed to the bed and knelt down beside it.

"Cyndi?" she whispered.

The uninterrupted rhythm of steady,

raspy breathing told her she hadn't pierced the confines of her friend's deep sleep.

"Hey. Cyn?" This time, she added a gentle nudge to the side of the mattress. "Cyndi?"

"Hmmm."

"Cyndi? Are you awake?"

"Huh?" Cyndi nuzzled against the pillow and then pushed her eyes open. "Whaddya want? Are you okay? Is it the hay?"

"What? No. I'm sorry to wake you," Lucy told her. "But did I hear you say the other day that you'd brought your laptop with you?"

"Yeah," she grunted.

"Would you mind if I borrowed it for a few minutes?"

The groan that followed was indecipherable, but Lucy decided to take it as permission.

"Great. Thank you."

"Uh-huh." Cyndi nuzzled the pillow again and closed her eyes.

"Wait," Lucy whispered. "I mean, could you tell me where it is?"

"I dunno," she replied with an irritable snarl. "On the dresser."

Lucy jumped to her feet and leaned over Cyndi, pulling the blanket up to her chin and tucking it in. "Thanks, Cyn."

On her way toward the dresser, Lucy banged her toe on the corner of the bed and let out a bark before slapping her hand across her mouth. When she found the laptop and picked it up, she didn't notice that it was plugged in, and she groaned as it yanked her backward.

"Lucy!" Cyndi howled. "Get out of here, would you?"

"Sorry, Cyn. Going now," she stammered as she wrapped the cord around her hand and backed up toward the door. "Sweet dreams."

Lucy was pulling the bedroom door closed when she heard Cyndi's muffled voice behind her.

"It doesn't work, by the way."

Lucy threw the door open again. "What?"

"There's no Internet connection except down in the lodge."

"Oh. Well, okay. Thanks."

Lucy flipped on the lamp in the living room and squinted to read the clock in the corner.

5:43 a.m.

Betty Sue had said she was always in the kitchen by six. Lucy crossed the cold floor again and let herself back into her bedroom long enough to feel around for a pair of jeans, a sweater, shoes, and socks. Fifteen minutes later, she was dressed and lugging Cyndi's laptop under her arm as she headed down the hill and toward the yellow light in the kitchen window.

"Can I come in?" she asked, and Betty Sue jumped in surprise.

"Sweet pea, you just about scared me silly."

"I'm sorry."

"Are you feeling all right?"

"Yeah, the Benadryl really helped. I just couldn't sleep, and Cyndi said you have an Internet connection down here."

"Sure do," she said, pointing to the desk in the corner. "Help yourself."

By the time the laptop was set up and Lucy had logged on, Betty Sue passed her a steaming cup of hot water and a tea bag.

"Thank you."

She typed in "Blanchard Springs Caverns," and the first ten of more than nineteen thousand possibilities came up on the screen. Lucy clicked on the first one and began to read about the living cave they would be visiting later that day.

"Is this why you couldn't sleep?" Betty Sue asked her, and Lucy tilted her head back to look at the woman standing behind her.

"Kinda."

"Claustrophobic?" she asked.

"Yeah."

"Just be sure to take the Dripstone Trail and not the Wild Cave Tour."

Lucy clicked on the Dripstone Trail link and read about the elevator ride that would take them two hundred feet down into the earth. The entire tour would only last an hour; she was pretty sure she could face just about anything for an hour.

She clicked on the Wild Cave Tour link, and she gasped as she read that visitors were expected to wear sturdy shoes and crawl on their hands and knees.

"Oh, man," she whimpered. "No thank you."

Lucy hurried to pack up the laptop, and she took another sip of tea before heading for the door.

"Thanks, Betty Sue. I'll see you at breakfast in a couple of hours."

"Get some sleep, sugar."

Lucy nodded, but she knew there was very little chance of that.

The sun was barely poking out its head for the day. The thermometer on the side of the lodge registered thirty-nine degrees, and several feet of mist hovered over the ground. Lucy pulled her sweater in around her as she jogged up the hill toward the cabin.

Just before she rounded the corner, a noise caught her attention, stopping Lucy in her tracks. She felt very much like a cartoon coyote, burning up the ground beneath her as she put on the brakes. If she weren't too terrified to look away, she'd have checked for the big black tire marks.

"Uh, okay, uh, stay. Stay right there."

A massive creature with tree-sized antlers raised its attention from the grass and looked back at her.

"I, uh, come in peace. Don't be startled, Mister Moose. Let's not make any sudden moves, either one of us."

Her heart was pounding so hard that all she could hear was the drumbeat in her ears. In slow motion, Lucy took one tiny step toward the cabin. When the creature didn't react, she ventured a second one.

But this time, the beast turned straight toward her, facing her head-on. He didn't make a move toward her, but the eye contact was intense and ominous, and Lucy couldn't help herself. In one swift motion, she tossed the laptop into the air, let out a long and bouncy shriek and ran for the cabin. Up the stairs and through the front door she scurried, still screaming as she slammed the door and bolted the lock.

"What is it?" Wendy shouted as she dashed out of the bedroom. "What happened?"

"M–m–moose," Lucy stuttered. "I was chased b–by a moose."

"A moose," Wendy repeated and then hurried to the window to look out. "Oh my goodness, it's an elk. Look at that!"

"Elk. Moose. Same thing. Scary and big."

"Are you sure it was chasing you? It looks pretty tame right now. It's just grazing."

"It looked me right in the eye," Lucy told her. "Threateningly."

Wendy giggled and then covered her mouth when Lucy shot her a betrayed frown.

"I'm sorry. I'm sure it was terrifying."

"It was."

Lucy took her first real look at Wendy, and she frowned.

No one looks this good straight out of bed. It's just not possible.

Wendy's silky blond tresses bounced upon her shoulders, and her skin was clear and radiant without makeup. She was dressed in a cropped pink sweatshirt and the cutest pink-and-gray-plaid flannel pajama bottoms that tied at the waist.

For crying out loud, her toenails even match, Lucy inwardly groaned when she noticed the iced pink polish on smooth, pedicured feet.

"What is that at the bottom of the steps?" Wendy asked, peering out the window again.

Lucy stepped up beside her at the window and gasped.

"Cyndi's laptop! I must have dropped it when I ran away."

"Oooooh, Lucy."

There it was on the ground, in three different chunks of plastic, glass, and connector cord.

"She's gonna hurt you bad," Wendy warned her.

"Oh yeah, she is," Lucy concurred with a groan.

She rushed into the bedroom and pulled her BlackBerry out of the pocket of her purse. Tossing herself to the bed, she began to enter a text.

SOS. Moose trouble. Broke C's laptop. Come right away.

"Mattie will know what to do," she announced.

A few moments later, the orange light in the corner of her BlackBerry illuminated, and a tone sounded to let her know a reply text had been received.

You need to stop using so much moose. Be right there.

* * * * *

The elk had wandered off by the time Matt arrived at the front door, several pieces of the laptop in his arms, and the connector cord draped around his neck. Lucy flung the door open, grabbed him by the arm, yanked him inside, slammed the door shut again, and set about bolting it.

"Were your hands slippery from putting mousse in your hair or something?" he asked, and Wendy burst into laughter.

"It was a *moose*, Mattie," she explained, raising her hands to either side of her head and spreading her fingers to demonstrate antlers.

Matt looked to Wendy, who stated, "It was an elk."

"A huge one!" Lucy exclaimed. "I was coming up the hill, and there he was. Blocking the door and staring at me, with those big, strange eyes."

"Luce, when was this?"

"This morning."

"What time?"

"I don't know. Six thirty?"

"What were you doing outside at six thirty this morning?"

"I went down to the lodge to use the internet connection."

Matt looked to Wendy, and she shrugged.

"I borrowed Cyndi's laptop so I could look something up. And when I came back, there he was, just standing there." She raised her hands again to create antlers, and she stared Matt down with dark, elk-like intensity. "I froze. I told him I didn't mean any harm and tried to take one step toward the cabin, and he looked like he was going to charge me."

"So he basically . . . flinched."

"Right."

"And that's when you threw the laptop at him to protect yourself."

"No, Mattie. I was scared, and I ran, and the laptop just . . . sort of . . . crashed to the ground. Can you fix it?"

Matt looked down at the broken computer and sighed. "No, Luce. I can't fix it."

"You have to."

They all appeared to have been placed on PAUSE as the door to the far bedroom creaked open and Cyndi stepped out into the room.

"What's going on?" she asked them, pulling her robe tightly shut when her sleepy eyes landed on Matt.

"Lucy was confronted by an elk," Wendy told her.

"It was terrifying," Lucy added.

Cyndi blinked several times and then squinted at Matt, tucking a wisp of short hair behind her ear.

"Is that— Hey! Is that *my laptop?!*"

* * * * *

Matt piled his plate with eggs, sausage, bacon, and two biscuits. Lucy was behind him in line, and he noticed a more demure approach on her part as she took scrambled eggs and fruit from the breakfast buffet before doubling back for a bagel and a cup of coffee.

"Sit with me," he said to her, and Lucy followed him to a vacant table and sat down beside him. "Are you okay?"

"I feel terrible about Cyndi's laptop," she admitted.

"She was pretty great about it, though."

"After the first twenty minutes of yelling at me."

"You'll replace it, and you've apologized. That's all you can do, Luce."

"I know. But I think I'll get her something additional to make up for it, too. Like maybe one of those great carrying bags."

"Nice. So tell me, what was so important that you were looking up this morning anyway?"

"I googled the caverns," she said and then raised her eyes from her plate. "They're pretty intense."

"Oh."

Matt had forgotten all about Lucy's penchant for oxygen.

Leaning in toward him, she whispered, "Betty Sue says there's a tour they offer in such a small space that you have to crawl on your hands and knees. We won't be taking that one, will we, Mattie?"

"Are there others?"

"Yeah, there's a more universal one called the Dripstone Trail where the walkways are wide, and it has hand railings and everything. I mean, you still have to go a couple of hundred feet into

209

the ground, but it only lasts an hour, so I think I could—"

Lucy fell silent the moment that Alison and Tony appeared, plates in hand.

"Can we join you?" Tony asked them.

"Of course. Sit down," Matt replied. "We were just talking about the caverns."

"It's going to be a trip, isn't it?" Tony said.

"I heard there's more than one tour that you can choose from," Matt said with a casual tone. "Which one are we taking?"

Wendy, Cyndi, and Justin joined the conversation just then, scraping back chairs and setting their plates on the table.

"There's a general tour," Alison said, "and then there's a far more intense one available where you crawl around and get dirty."

"Let's crawl around and get dirty," Wendy piped up, and Matt felt Lucy deflate in the chair next to him.

"Oh yeah, let's go intense," Justin said on a chuckle, and he and Wendy shared a high-five.

"I'm not really up for a cavern crawl," Matt told them and then popped a chunk of biscuit into his mouth. "I think I'd like to take the general tour, if no one minds."

"We can split up then," Alison decided. "Let me find out how many want the Wild Cave Tour and how many want the Dripstone Trail, and I'll call and confirm the reservation with the changes."

"I'm with Mattie," Lucy said, and Justin groaned.

"No way, Lucy. Come with us. It'll be an adventure."

"I don't want Matt to go alone," she said, and her eyes met Matt's as she smiled. "He wouldn't let me go alone, if the shoe was on the other foot."

"Cowards, both of you," Justin teased, but by the time the final count was taken, only four opted for the wilder version, and cowards were in the majority.

"Wendy, Justin, Jeff, and Tony," Alison recapped. "And the rest of us will embark on the bunny slope tour."

Justin raised an eyebrow at Lucy. "Last chance, girl. Come with us."

Matt waited, wondering if she would give in and face one of her deepest fears just to impress him.

"Nope. I don't think so," she replied,

and Matt's faith in her was restored for the moment.

Justin sighed and draped his arm loosely around Wendy's shoulder.

"Looks like it's just you and me, Wen," he said.

Matt noticed that Lucy's face was as unreadable as a china plate, but her private disappointment was palpable to him.

"Okay, then," Alison announced. "We have the morning free, and we'll meet back here to pick up our box lunches at noon. We'll head out to the caverns after that. Any questions?"

When they dispersed, Matt followed Lucy out the door and touched her arm. "Want to go for a hike or something?"

"Nah," she replied. "I think I'm going to grab my journal and my Bible and take some time for myself that doesn't involve movement."

They walked on in silence until they reached the first cabin.

"This is my stop," Lucy said with a halfhearted smile. "I'll see you later."

Matt thought of a dozen things he wanted to say, but something in his spirit drew it all back. Instead, he nodded and cuffed Lucy's arm playfully before he headed up the hill toward his own cabin.

"Hey, Mattie," she called, and he turned to face her. "Thanks for coming so quickly this morning."

"No worries."

She lifted one shoulder in half a shrug and graced him with a fraction of a smile before climbing the stairs and disappearing inside.

Oh, Lord.

I feel like such a fool right now. My heart just aches, and I'm about as unsure and out of my element as I ever remember being.

Am I crazy? Have I latched on to the first hot guy to cross my path just because there's no one else on my horizon at the moment? Did You send Justin as an answer to my prayers, or did I grab him and force him into that role just because I like the way he looks?

I am the exact opposite of everything he says he wants in a woman. I'm not at home on a campground or in the river or on top of a horse. He's an adventurer, a risk-taker—and the biggest risk I take is wearing flats with evening wear.

But if Justin's not The One, what hope do I have for meeting someone to make a life with? Am I going to be alone for the rest of my life?

I came to Snowball so certain, so sure. All I had to do was put myself into situations that Justin enjoyed and You would do the rest. But so far I've been terrorized by a demon fish, bitten by flesh-eating insects, tortured by a freakishly wide horse, stalked by an elk, and tormented by hay. Now I'm being sent to an underground death trap, and Justin isn't even going to be there! Instead, he'll be crawling around in small spaces with the fair-haired, perfect-footed Wendy. Are you trying to tell me something here?

Certainly, not every woman was born excited about dangling a worm on a hook or being buried alive, but eventually they do it. I have to believe it's because they try it and learn to love it. Like me and basketball. I never thought I could enjoy watching sports, but I went to one Razorbacks game with Mattie and George and I was hooked. That can happen with something Justin loves, right?

If Justin and I have a future, I hope You'll begin to let me know. Because so far I've been just about as grossed-out, muscle-worn, and terrified as I can handle.

Still hoping,
Lucy Binoche

Chapter Eleven

THE ELEVATOR GROANED DOWN INTO THE depths of the earth, and when the doors opened, two tour guides and five members of the Bender family joined Matt, Lucy, Alison, Cyndi, Rob, and Brenda as they stepped into a vastness that the guide called the Cathedral Room.

Lucy wheezed as she drew air in through her nose and down into her lungs.

"There's plenty of air in this cavern," Matt whispered, and she knew he was right. But it didn't help in the least.

"The temperature in this area," the

older of the two guides told them, "is kept to a constant fifty-eight degrees. Humidity, as you've probably noticed, is one hundred percent."

Lucy had noticed.

"Along the way, you may spot additional visitors, such as salamanders, crickets, bats, and the like."

"Dude," one of the Bender boys commented to his cousin, "it's like the Bat Cave."

Wide, paved trails flanked with masonry curbs and handrails led them through the limestone caves. From the Cathedral Room and the Giant Column of colorful formations to the pure calcite formations in the Coral Room, the surroundings were magnificent.

When she wasn't gulping air, Lucy had to admit that the cavern wasn't something she would have chosen to miss. Her favorite sight was the Coral Pond, with delicate lacy patterns formed underneath the shallow water.

"Mattie, look at that. It's incredible. It just really reminds you how great our God is, doesn't it?"

For several minutes at a time, Lucy

marveled at her ability to forget that she was underground. Sparkling flowstone, towering columns, and delicate soda straws kept her fascinated.

"I'm proud of you," Matt whispered as they climbed the steep incline of the path, and it brought a grin to her face.

"Thanks. Me too, kinda."

The tour guide led them to a seating area where they took a break and listened to detailed explanations about the formations before them. Lucy overheard one of the boys say that he wanted to take a keepsake from the cavern home with him.

"We hear that a lot," the guide said. "But think about how quickly these incredible formations would disappear if every visitor followed through on that."

Lucy let out a sudden scream as a large, thick object came out of nowhere and whacked her right in the middle of the forehead.

"Whoa! Dude, did you see that?" one of the Bender boys asked.

"What *was* that?" Lucy asked while rubbing her forehead.

"How cool was that?" exclaimed Ty, the

youngest of the three boys. "Lady, you got hit in the head by a bat."

Lucy's first thought was to wonder why someone would bring a baseball bat along on such an outing. But as realization began to dawn, panic rose within her.

"Bats are fairly rare in this part of the cavern," the guide told them. "But it's mating season in the area, so every now and then in the winter months we'll see a few of them."

"Ewww," Brenda moaned.

"I know," Cyndi agreed.

"That being said," the guide added, "you almost never see one mis-navigate that way. Bats are equipped with a type of inner sonar, and—"

"Wait a minute," Lucy exclaimed, popping to her feet. "A bat? *A BAT* just flew into my head?"

"Settle down, Luce," Matt said softly, just a moment too late.

Before she knew what she was going to do, Lucy pushed her way past the row of people seated next to her and took off at a full run.

"Ma'am, please stay with the group."

"Let me out of here!" she screamed, tumbling as she ran down the trail.

"Dude, she's crying like your little sister!" one of the teenagers declared.

Lucy ignored the burn on the palm of her hand as it scraped along the ground, and she began scrambling so hard to make it back to her feet again that she plunked down one more time.

"Lucy, it's okay," Matt said, as he placed both hands under her arms and lifted her to her feet again.

"Mattie, I can't. I can't. I can't breathe."

"I know. It's going to be okay. One of the guides is going to take us back up."

"Now," she gasped. "I need to go now."

The cavern began swirling around her, and when something thumped against her arm, Lucy cried out and swatted it as hard as she could.

"Hey!" Matt exclaimed. "I'm not a bat!"

"S—sorry," she managed before diving into the steel car. "Close the door." Grabbing the young guide with both hands, Lucy shrieked, "Let's go, let's go, let's go."

* * * * *

It was bad enough that most of the singles had a front row seat for her meltdown, but Lucy also had to spend the entire hour's ride back to the campsite listening to the story as it was recounted to Justin and Jeff. Matt knew it must be killing her.

"Our tour was one of the most amazing adventures I've ever been on," Justin told them. "But I'd almost give it up to witness that!"

"You should have seen it," Cyndi told them. "It just came out of nowhere and dove straight at Lucy and banged her right in the middle of her head."

"Yeah, and one of the teenagers on the tour with us," Brenda added, "turns to Lucy and says, 'Dude. You got hit in the head by a bat.'"

Lucy clamped her eyes shut as the roar of laughter kicked in again, and Matt resisted the urge to reach out and pat her arm.

The attendant at the first-aid station had checked her thoroughly for bite marks, and he seemed to feel he was comforting Lucy by assuring her that rabies shots wouldn't be necessary. As she tried to control the hyperventilating that the news evoked, the attendant had treated the

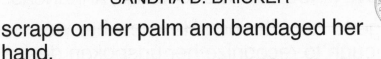

scrape on her palm and bandaged her hand.

Even though the skin luckily hadn't been broken, Lucy's forehead was still emblazoned with a large red mark, and her face wore the expression of a whipped dog on a leash. Looking at her just about broke Matt's heart.

When they arrived back at the retreat site, Lucy was the first one out of their car. Seizing the opportunity, Matt called to the others for their attention.

"Hey," he snapped. "I think she's had enough now. Let's try to be a little compassionate, huh?"

"We're just teasing her," Brenda defended.

"And I think we've mastered that. How about we just be her friends now?"

Matt didn't wait for their reactions before climbing out of the car. Lucy was already heading up the hill as Alison called them all toward the lodge for dinner.

"Luce?" Matt called to her. "Don't you want to come and eat something?"

"Not hungry, Mattie." She didn't even look back at him, and Matt resisted the urge to run after her. He knew her well enough to recognize her unspoken desire to spend some time alone to regroup.

By the time Matt had filled his plate and joined the others at the table, Lucy's adventure was being detailed yet again, this time for Wendy, who had ridden back in the other car.

"She's had a tough day, hasn't she?" Wendy sympathized. "It started out with the elk, and now this."

"What elk?" Brenda piped up. "Are you telling us that Lucy had a run-in with yet another member of the wildlife community today? The girl is a drama magnet!"

Her raspy laughter rubbed Matt the wrong way. He dropped his fork to his plate and scuffed back his chair.

"Okay. I think we've enjoyed more than enough laughter at Lucy's expense."

"Oh, come on, Matt," Brenda said. "Lighten up. You have to admit that this is all pretty hilarious."

"Not to Lucy, it's not," he replied. He got up from the table, leaving his dinner behind.

"It's not like she's here to hear us."

"Matt, come on," Justin called after him.

But Matt kept on walking. He didn't want to risk saying something he might later regret.

* * * * *

Lucy stood in front of the foggy bathroom mirror and stared at herself. The redness was nearly gone from her forehead, and the bug bites were now imperceptible. But that huge slap of embarrassment stained across her cheeks and chest was unmistakable.

She ran her fingers through her thick, wet curls several times and then combed them back into a ponytail that she clasped with a thick blue band. Wrapping herself in a soft terry towel, Lucy opened the door and padded toward her bedroom to throw on some sweats.

She poked the earphones from her iPod headset into her ears and flipped on some music. Then she leaned both pillows against the headboard and settled back into them with a can of diet soda, a snack pack of Oreos, and one of Wendy's Christian romance novels on her lap. Two chapters and four cookies later, she was feeling a little better as Wendy creaked open the door and stuck her head through.

"Can I come in?"

Lucy pulled out her earphones and turned the book facedown on her knee.

"If you don't feel like talking, I don't want to bother you," Wendy told her. "But I brought you a doggie bag from dinner."

"What did you have?"

"Barbecued chicken."

Lucy smiled and motioned Wendy inside with a wiggling index finger.

"Oooooh," she cooed as she peeled back the lid from the plastic container. "Mac and cheese?"

"A comfort food supper, Betty Sue called it."

"Except for the string beans."

"Right. Can I get you something to drink?"

Lucy motioned to the diet soda on the nightstand, and Wendy smiled.

"You're all set then. I can leave you alone."

"No. Stay."

"You're sure?"

She nodded, and Wendy scooted back on the bed and leaned against the wall.

"How are you liking that?" she asked when she caught sight of the romance novel. "I finished it last night. It's one of my new favorites."

"I needed a nice diversion. I hope you don't mind."

"Not at all. You've had a pretty rough day, haven't you?"

Lucy tried to laugh. "As my aunt Trudy used to say, it's been like trying to swim the English Channel strapped to a cannon."

Wendy chuckled as Lucy took a big bite out of the chicken thigh.

"She had a bunch of sayings like that. 'Like climbing Mount Everest on roller skates.' Or, 'That was as much fun as having a peanut butter dumpling for dinner.'"

Wendy's chuckle rolled into full-fledged laughter, and Lucy couldn't help but join her.

"I don't know if you've noticed, but I'm not exactly an outdoorsy type of girl."

Wendy lifted her eyes and grinned. "Not everyone is."

"I'm a disaster, actually. But I got this idea in my head that I wanted to conquer these aversions."

"Why?"

"Oh, it's too embarrassing to tell you," she admitted.

"Well, I admire the attempt anyway. It's impressive."

"Yeah," Lucy said with a hint of sarcasm. "I'll bet you'd have really been impressed today when I went flying out of the Bat Cave, shrieking."

"I'm not entirely sure I wouldn't have done the same thing if a bat had flown into my head, Lucy."

"That poor tour guide," she said with a laugh. "I grabbed him by the shoulders and started shaking him, screaming for him to get me out of there."

They were both laughing so hard that Lucy had to set her dinner aside. And when Wendy let out a snort, they both fell over on their sides, cackling like hysterical hens.

When they were finally able to pull themselves together and sit upright again, Lucy sniffed and shook her head.

"You know, Wendy, I'm glad Alison roomed us together."

"Me too, Lucy. It's really been fun."

"I wasn't so sure it was a good idea in the beginning," Lucy admitted.

"Why?"

"Well, you're just so perfect. No one wants to be constantly reminded of her own imperfections."

Wendy snickered. "I'm not perfect."

"No? Name one flaw."

"My hair, for one," Wendy told her, twisting her hair around her fist and pulling it toward her.

"Your hair! Please! It's like silk."

"Straight and lifeless, more like," she corrected. "*You* are the one with perfect hair."

"Are you kidding? I can't get it to settle down and fly right for anything."

"You don't want it to settle down, Lucy. That's the beauty of having all those natural curls."

"Just once, I'd like to see myself with straight, silky hair."

"Well, that's why God made straightening irons, my friend. I even use one on my hair now and then."

"You do? Do you have it with you?"

"Sure do."

"Sometime before the week is up, would you straighten my hair for me? Just to see what it looks like?"

229

"Of course. But you won't like it."

"I'll be the judge of that."

They shared another smile, and Wendy reached out and patted Lucy's hand.

"Anything I can get you before I grab a shower?"

"No, thanks."

"Are you coming to devotions tonight? Or have you had enough of us today?"

"I might. I thought I'd just rest for a while and see how I feel."

"Good idea."

Lucy watched her leave the room, marveling at the affection for Wendy that filled her heart. She suddenly regarded Wendy as someone she wanted to continue a friendship with, someone she could see herself hanging out with, chatting about work with, laughing with.

And then she thought of Justin.

For a moment, Lucy allowed herself to wonder whether Wendy was actually a better match for him than she herself would be. But a fresh supply of confidence came out of nowhere, and Lucy was reminded of the initial flyer Alison had created to solicit singles to sign up for the retreat.

RELAX. RENEW. REFRESH.
AND SEEK HIS WILL FOR YOUR LIFE.

She had come to Snowball determined to put her best foot forward with Justin, to play out the entire weeklong retreat and see how things turned out.

Okay, so things weren't swimming along. There had been a snafu or two along the way. But like Scarlet O'Hara's life at Tara, tomorrow was always another day.

"You look better, by the way," Wendy said, as she came back into the room.

"I feel better," Lucy told her. "I've decided to put today behind me and start fresh tomorrow. The worst really does have to be behind me now, right?"

"Right!" Wendy exclaimed in support.

"The activities Alison planned have hit every one of my problem areas already. What else could there be? I mean, unless it's bungee jumping off some tall building, I think I'm good to go."

"Excellent."

"So what does she have planned for tomorrow, do you think?"

"Let's see," Wendy said as she

rummaged through the papers on the nightstand beside her bed. "Here we go. Tomorrow, we . . . oh."

"Not bungee jumping," Lucy inquired with caution.

"No."

"Good. What then?"

"Um. Hot air balloons."

Lucy fell backward onto her pillows and covered her face with one of them as she let out a muffled scream.

I woke up in the middle of the night, just before I crashed to the ground after falling six-thousand feet off the side of a mountain. In a dream, of course.

Gee, I can't imagine why I'm dreaming about falling from great heights.

Why, Lord, why? Why? WHY??

Why didn't I read the calendar of events beforehand?

Why didn't I just try to bond with Justin over coffee and stale donuts before Sunday services instead of coming on this ridiculous thrill ride of a retreat?

And most importantly, why am I afraid of everything on the earth?

What is wrong with me? Why can't I be an adventurer like Wendy? She crawled around the "Wild" portion of that cave visit until her jeans were clay-colored from hip to knee. And not once did a maniacal bat swoop down and smack her in the head while she did it. Why does she have to be so cool and I have to be so . . . ME?

PLEASE don't let me embarrass myself today by fainting or screaming or falling out of the balloon. Bless me with Your peace and calmness and turn me into a normal human being, if just for a few hours, Lord.

Either that, or give me a nice big rainstorm so the ballooning is canceled? That's not too much to ask, right? Or maybe some hail.

Watching for a blizzard,
Lucy

Chapter Twelve

"THE BUFFALO NATIONAL RIVER WAS FIRST designated a National River in nineteen-seventy-two," Alison read to them from the brochure. "It comprises one-hundred-thirty-five miles of floatable river and protected wilderness. Serenely float in a wicker basket high above the magnificent scenery for an unparalleled view of a lifetime."

"Serenely float," Lucy repeated to Matt. "That sounds good, right? Serenity isn't a description that usually precedes the tale of four people plummeting to their deaths."

"Settle down, girl. There will be no plummeting today," Matt promised, and Lucy made a silent agreement that ended in "Amen," suddenly turning it into a prayer.

They all stood back and watched in the distance as two hot air balloon canvasses were unrolled on the dewy morning grass. A chill meandered from the base of Lucy's spine to the nape of her neck as large fans began filling the balloons with air. Heat generated by burners slowly raised the multicolored balloons to attention before them. Lucy figured they were each six or seven stories tall, and she looked up at the one on the right, imagining herself in the wicker basket beneath it, floating through the sky.

"Luce? Are you all right?" Matt asked in low-toned concern.

"Fine. Just a little woozy." *A lot woozy, but who's measuring?*

"Okay, let's break up into groups of five," Alison suggested.

"I–I'm not going," Cyndi announced. "I've been thinking about it, and I'm just not going."

"Oh, Cyn, come on," Rob urged, but

she was emphatic, shaking her head at a frantic rhythm.

"No. I'm not going. I am not going."

Lucy understood. Deeply. She reached over and squeezed Cyndi's hand, giving her a nod.

I feel you, Cyndi.

Then Alison did something she almost never did. Alison adjusted.

"All right then. We'll go five and four."

"I want to go with Lucy," Wendy told them. "Matt and Justin, you want to go with us?"

Alison looked at her clipboard and gave a slight pinch to her face before agreeing. "That works."

"Great."

Lucy caught Wendy's grin and returned it before following her across the grass toward one of the two waiting monstrosities, reminding herself that people did this all the time.

With Wendy and Matt both thinking good and safe and positive thoughts about the ride ahead, Lucy felt like she stood a chance of keeping it together so that Justin need never know how frightening it was for her to put more than a few yards between the soles of her shoes and the precious, stable ground.

After Lucy climbed aboard, she noticed Cyndi standing at the sidelines. She recognized that look in Cyndi's eyes, too. Fear mixed with disappointment in herself for not conquering it.

"Cyn!" Lucy called out to her. "If I can, you can."

Cyndi's head tilted tentatively. Lucy and Wendy both motioned with their hands to call her toward them. At first Cyndi didn't move a muscle, but suddenly she let out a loud scream and took off running toward them.

The occupants of both balloons erupted into applause as Cyndi crossed the wet grass and climbed over the side of the gondola to embrace Wendy and Lucy.

"I'm so proud of you," Lucy told her through a mist of emotion. "I understand, I really do."

"This is going to be so much fun," Wendy seemed to promise them both. "And we're always going to remember that we did it together."

Justin dragged Matt into a comical

240

embrace, repeating the sentiment in a high-pitched voice. "It's true, Matt. We'll always remember that we did this together."

Matt pushed him away, laughing.

"Come on!" Justin exclaimed, shaking Cyndi by both shoulders. "This is an adventure. Let the adrenaline flow!"

Lucy noticed Alison waving and, as she started to wave back, she noticed the ground drifting away. The balloons had already been untethered, and they were floating upward while her stomach dropped in the opposite direction. The balloon overhead heaved a deep sigh.

Pthhhhhhhht.

John, their guide, busied himself with the flight, and Lucy reached over and clutched the side of the gondola.

A cape of early morning fog enveloped them, the promise of blue skies reaching from the horizon. In snippets through the clouds, Lucy caught sight of patches of green grass, canopy nets of crimson-leafed trees, and a thick, curvy snake of dark green waters.

"It's beautiful," Wendy said on a sigh.

Pthhhhhhhht.

Lucy jumped as the balloon groaned again.

"It's just about the most personal look you can get of the Buffalo," John told them.

"How long have you been at this?" Justin asked him.

"Ten years of amazing rides," he replied. "The world and her problems are much smaller from this vantage point."

"I can see that."

Lucy grasped the side of the basket a little tighter and held on, leaning against Matt for further security. To her right, Wendy moved close to her and they locked arms. Then Lucy reached out with her left arm and pulled Cyndi into the fold.

"How are you doing?" Matt asked over her shoulder. "You okay?"

Lucy simply nodded. She couldn't manage to look away from hundred-foot cliffs that framed the Buffalo below them, or from the fishermen that looked like small, colorful beans along the riverbanks.

The wind moved them northward, and she noticed her knees growing weak as the balloon dropped gracefully.

"We're dropping! Are we falling?" Cyndi cried.

"No worries, little lady," John reassured her, and Lucy clung to the promise as well. "In just a minute, you'll get a bird's-eye view."

They floated along the treetops, and Lucy held her breath as Wendy released her arm and leaned forward to touch a sprig of leaves. She heard the continuous *click-click-click* of Matt's camera from behind her, and Lucy started to wonder if God had answered her prayers about not making a fool of herself. There she was, after all, standing on her own (albeit trembling) legs, gliding across hilltops, trees, rocky cliffs, and emerald waters, and she was still upright. She hadn't fainted or fallen or so much as rocked the basket. Her breathing was almost normal, and no one had been hurt, including herself.

It's kind of a miracle, she realized. *Thank You, Lord.*

Lucy gazed at Justin, and the soft, warm smile he gave her seemed to stroke her cheeks with velvet fingers. He was really the most beautiful man she'd ever seen up close. The breeze caused his hair to dance a bit, and Lucy noticed golden flecks in his eyes that reflected the morning sun.

"This is fantastic," he told her, and he slid his arm around Lucy's shoulder and gave her a gentle hug.

A thousand feet above the ground, with Justin's muscular arm around her, Lucy felt a little like the wind had been let out of her.

"It really is," she managed, but it came out in a whimper. "It's breathtaking."

The morning had made her bold, and Lucy decided to make a daring and audacious move. Biting her lip, she tilted her head slightly and let it rest on Justin's shoulder. Just for a moment, and not the full weight of it, but it rested there just the same.

Justin gave her arm a squeeze, and Lucy thought for a moment that she was in heaven. She smiled at the literal truth of it as she floated along in the sky, her head on the shoulder of the man of her dreams, the spicy scent of him mixing with brisk, fresh air and sweet autumn trees.

"You know what they say," John declared. "What goes up must come down, right?"

Lucy's head bobbed upright immediately and she slipped out of Justin's embrace as the final *pthhhhhhhht* overhead squeezed her insides.

"What's happening?" Cyndi asked, her dark eyes large and round as the top of a question mark, and Lucy shook her head.

"I don't know."

"See that plot of grass over there?" John asked, pointing out a miniscule square of land in the distance. "That's where we're going to come down."

Lucy's heart began to race.

"Shouldn't there be a runway or something?" she asked, looking from Justin to Wendy to Matt and then back at the guide.

"John's done this a thousand times," Matt reminded her.

"Yeah, but—" Lucy's words escaped her, and her mouth hung gaping open in the shape of a large, round *O*.

Suddenly, the ride no longer epitomized peaceful abandon. In fact, the closer the tiny plot of earth came toward them, the less peace Lucy could manage to grab hold of with her two fists and clenched teeth.

"It's okay," John assured her. "You'll hardly feel the landing."

But Lucy didn't believe him, proof of which was the morning's eggs and bacon bouncing on a trampoline inside her stomach as a falling sensation set her head to spinning.

"Are you sure you can land in that little space?" Cyndi asked.

Lucy closed her eyes tight and tried to pray that he could, but the prayer wouldn't quite come.

"Lucy?" Matt inquired.

"I don't feel so good," she told him, right before she leaned over the side of the gondola and sent the remains of her breakfast spilling down into the trees.

So much for Matt's prediction about no plummeting that day.

* * * * *

Lucy pulled the blanket over her head and tucked her entire body underneath it. Forget that there was no air, forget that she didn't like closed-in spaces, forget that the tiny world beneath that blanket was closing in on her.

"Sugar?"

She yanked the blanket down to her chin and peered out.

"Are you all right, darlin'?"

Betty Sue stood in the doorway, holding a tray and wearing a crooked, sympathetic smile that made Lucy want to crawl back under the blanket.

"I guess you heard."

"I did."

Betty Sue set the tray down on the ottoman at the foot of the bed and perched on a corner of the mattress.

"Justin has convinced everyone that it was too much of my smokehouse bacon from this morning's buffet. But that wasn't it, was it?"

"No," Lucy whimpered. "It wasn't the bacon."

"I didn't think so."

Lucy sensed their untimely arrival a fraction of a second before the tears made their way up and over the edges of her eyes and cascaded down her cheeks.

"Do you want to have a chat, sugar?"

Lucy didn't have an answer for that one.

"Well, why don't I do the chattin'," Betty Sue suggested, nudging Lucy with her elbow. "You prop up those pillows behind you and have a little soup. You can't go all day without anything on your stomach."

Lucy wasn't the least bit hungry, but she summoned up the courtesy instilled in her from a young age and did as she was told. Betty Sue lowered the tray to her lap. Chicken broth, saltine crackers, and iced ginger ale were all the right offerings for an upset stomach and a bruised ego.

Betty Sue lifted the soup spoon from its place atop a folded linen napkin and handed it to Lucy. When she took it, the woman smiled and smoothed back Lucy's hair.

"I've learned a thing or two from my years in the service of people," she said, her kindness washing over Lucy and turning her insides to a sort of warm putty. "And it can all pretty much be boiled down to one idea."

Lucy slurped at the soup and then raised her eyes with eager anticipation.

"Do you want to know what that is?"

She nodded.

"Everybody's got somethin'."

Lucy narrowed her eyes and furrowed her brow as she waited for more. When Betty Sue made no move to expound, Lucy set down her spoon and regarded the woman curiously.

"More?" Betty Sue asked.

"Please."

"Take your church group, for instance. Alison, well, she's got leadership."

Lucy snorted, nodding in agreement.

"She carries around her clipboard with all her notes about where to go and what to do and how to organize it all. That's what she's got. Now, Brenda, she doesn't have that."

"No," Lucy agreed.

"Brenda's a watcher and a listener. She sees and hears every little thing that goes on around her. She stores it up and saves it for later."

"When she's sure to tell anyone who will listen."

Betty Sue chuckled at that. "Sure enough." She paused to break a few crackers into the bowl of broth before continuing. "Rob, he's analytical. He's a smart boy—could probably figure out just about anything if he worked at the puzzle long enough."

Lucy hadn't thought of Rob that way, but it was right on. Not that she knew Rob all that well, but she was fascinated that Betty Sue could so easily perceive that quality in him.

"Justin, now. He's got the looks."

Lucy let out a sudden pop of a giggle. "Yes. He sure does."

"And Matthew has that heart of his."

Matt's heart *was* his best attribute. It was kind, understanding, and enormous.

"Do you see where I'm going here, sugar?"

"Not really."

"Everybody's got somethin'," she repeated. "And there's no shame in not having the something that somebody else has, because you've got something of your own."

"Oh."

She felt a flush of embarrassed heat

move up her neck and straight over the top of her head. Betty Sue took Lucy's hand between both of hers, and as she stroked it, Lucy noticed the wrinkled skin and short, clipped nails in contrast to her own younger, smoother hand.

"Why don't you tell me why you're working so hard to be someone you're not instead of embracing the beautiful woman God made you to be."

Betty Sue's eyes were kind—two blue pools that decorated her suntanned face—and they looked straight into Lucy and sweetly tweaked her heart.

"I'm just so—" Lucy couldn't complete the thought before the tears began to fall again.

"You're so what, sugar?"

"Insignificant."

She didn't expect the chortle of a laugh that came out of Betty Sue, and Lucy wiped her eyes with the back of her hand.

"Insignificant?" she asked her, plucking several tissues out of the box on the nightstand and handing them to Lucy. "Where on earth would you get an idea like that?"

"I'm afraid of—or allergic to—everything, Betty Sue. I have no talents, and there's nothing special about me."

"That's not true," came a deep voice from behind them.

Both of the women turned to find Matt standing in the doorway.

"There is so much about you that is special, Luce. I wish you could see that."

"Oh, Mattie, come on. I'm afraid of big animals, like *horses*! And mooses. O–or *moose*. I'm afraid of suffocating in dark, airless places. And having my feet more than a couple of yards off the ground makes me want to . . . well . . . you know."

Matt crossed the room and sat down on the edge of Wendy's bed, propping an ankle up on his knee. Betty Sue smoothed Lucy's hair again, and Lucy found herself wishing she still had a mom to share moments like this one with.

"I don't know how to fish or row a boat or . . . or . . . even pick out a pair of tennis shoes that feel good on my feet!"

"And this makes you insignificant, how?" Betty Sue asked her.

"In comparison to everybody else I'm just useless, Betty Sue."

The woman shook her silver head and thumped Lucy's blanket-padded leg. Lucy glanced at Matt, and he was shaking his head in much the same manner.

"*Useless.* That's a mighty stern word to use about yourself," Betty Sue told her. "And it seems a little ungrateful, which I never would have pegged you for being."

"Ungrateful?"

"It indicates to me that you've ignored the many beautiful qualities that our Father crafted especially in you. Like your kind heart. And your sense of humor. And the way you took to cooking when you said you'd never had much practice before. That was evidence of a chef in the making, if you ask me."

"Really?"

"And the way you notice every little thing, like the flowers in the vases down at the lodge," Matt chimed in.

"That shows me there's a nurturer in you," Betty Sue told her. "You're someone who sees the beauty in the details."

Excitement rose up inside of Lucy at

that, her eyes darting from Betty Sue to Matt and back again. "That's what I always say, isn't it, Mattie? In my work at the Conroy. I always say that the beauty of a memorable visit is in the details."

"And you're right. Dave and I adopted that idea long ago, and it's proven itself to be true, time and time again."

Lucy took a sip of the ginger ale and then set the tray aside.

"Do you see what I'm saying to you here, sugar?"

"I think so."

"God gave each one of us something special, and reaching for what we *want* to be good at rather than cultivating what we were *meant* to be good at is just going to end up in disappointment. If somebody doesn't love you because you can't catch a fish or because high places make you lose your breakfast, then they're not seeing you for the beautiful, nurturing, sweet potato bisque master chef that you are."

Lucy chuckled and rubbed Betty Sue's arm briskly.

"Thank you."

"Any time. Will I see you at devotions in the lodge tonight?"

"I think so."

"Good. Because we're having a very special fondue for dessert."

"Fondue?"

"Strawberries and pineapple, with chocolate for dipping."

"I'm there."

"Now, Matt, why don't you come with me and let your friend get some rest before she has to change out of those sweats of hers."

Matt followed Betty Sue through the door and then paused, turning back toward Lucy without a word.

"What?" she asked him.

"Just tell him, Luce. Tell him you can't ride a Ferris wheel, much less a hot air balloon. That you're no outdoorsman but you have other qualities he might like just as much once you show them to him. Just tell the truth about who you are."

Lucy lowered her eyes and twisted a loose thread on the blanket around her index finger without answering.

"Because who you are is pretty great,"

he told her. "If he can't see that, he doesn't deserve you."

Blinking back a mist of tears to which she was determined not to surrender, she raised a crooked, tight-lipped smile.

"Thanks, Mattie. I'll see you later."

Thank You for sending Betty Sue to me today, Lord. I really heard everything she and Mattie had to say, and I recognize the Source of the message. I really do. I'm going to try to just see if Justin is interested in the real Lucy.

This morning in the balloon, B.B. (Before Barfing), we had a spectacular moment where he put his arm around me and I laid my head on his shoulder. For just that instant, everything in life was perfect. It felt as if Justin returned what I was feeling for him and I wasn't just some crazy woman semi-stalking a guy she has no possible chance of landing.

So from now on, it's the Real Lucy. Let's see how she plays in Snowball, Arkansas.

Old and Improved,
Lucy B.

Chapter Thirteen

IT TOOK JUST OVER AN HOUR TO GET FROM Snowball to the town of Mountain View, and for the last half hour of the drive, Alison read aloud everything she'd learned about the place on the Internet.

One of the Dream Towns of the area, population less than three thousand.

Oozing with hand-hewn rusticity, rural charm, and down-home hospitality.

Fiddling and picking downtown on the square.

Lucy didn't want to hate the little town just because Alison had pushed her into knowing too much about it before they ever arrived, but she was convinced that she was really going to have to work against it.

The good news was, she was wrong.

The place was so charming that she'd forgotten all about Alison and her traveling *Mountain View 101* class the minute they all climbed out of the cars and set out for a walk down Main Street.

"The activities list was kind to me today, Mattie," she declared as she pointed toward an antique store across from the square. "Shopping is something at which I can no doubt excel."

"And possibly instruct others about, as well," Matt added with a grin.

"Wait, wait," Alison called out, as everyone separated into different directions. "We're meeting back here on the square at one o'clock."

Justin's enthusiasm bubbled over as he jogged toward a shop with camping gear in the window display. He was like a heat-seeking missile with its course firmly set, and Lucy shrugged as she headed down the street at Matt's side.

Meandering through the antique store, they admired a carved, vintage wardrobe and several exquisite sofas and settees. A crystal lamp with a cut-glass dome spoke to Lucy, but she was able to silence the call with one look at the price tag.

"If I stumbled upon a windfall or something and I could start up my own hotel like the Conroy," Lucy declared, "I would furnish it from this store."

"When you trip over that million," Matt suggested, "why don't you buy a B and B somewhere between the mountains and the city, and we can run it together."

"It's a deal. You take care of the books and the business end of things, and I'll be in charge of creating the style."

"A match made in heaven."

They were mutually drawn toward an overhead sign that promised fine arts and crafts from local artists, and the pledge did not disappoint. Lucy and Matt didn't emerge from the store again for more than an hour.

"Hey, look!" she exclaimed. "Cappuccino. Let's go over and have one, Mattie."

Matt's cell phone jingled with an arriving text message just as they reached the bistro. "Go ahead," Lucy told him. "Get us a seat and take that. I'll grab a couple of coffees."

"Latte with—"

"—a double shot of espresso," she finished for him. "I know."

Lucy had just ordered Matt's latte and her half-caf skinny vanilla cappuccino when Wendy, Justin, and Tony walked up beside her.

"Matt and I are getting some coffee. Want to join us?" she asked them.

"Sounds like a plan," Justin said.

"We're by the sidewalk," Lucy told them, taking the paper cups from counter. "Come on over when you've ordered."

Matt was typing a text message when she found the table and sat down across from him.

"Sedgewick," he told her as he completed the message.

"Look who I found." Lucy nodded toward the counter. "They're going to join us in a minute."

"Good."

Lucy leaned back into the padded chair and nursed her coffee cup while Matt finished tapping out another message back to George. He nodded to the others as they approached, and Justin pulled a nearby table next to theirs.

"We found the sweetest little bookstore down the street," Wendy said as she plopped an overloaded bag down on the seat of an empty chair. "I spent less than fifty dollars for all of this."

"Where is it?"

"I'll take you there when we're through, if you'd like."

"Luce, Sedgewick's got a line on Razorbacks tickets next Wednesday night. Are you in?"

"You bet."

Wendy looked at her curiously. "Razorbacks?"

"Basketball."

"Really!"

"Yep," Lucy replied with a shrug. "Who are they playing?"

"San Antonio," Justin interjected. "My hometown."

"Are you going?" Matt asked.

"Yeah. Great seats, too. The closest to courtside that I've ever scored."

"We should organize a drive out to Fayetteville together then."

"That works. My buddy has an Explorer. I'll get him to drive."

Lucy's heart began to pound. She could kiss Matt for that!

"I'm a little surprised that you're a fan of basketball, Lucy," Tony commented.

"Oh? Why? It's not like I have to watch from a hot air balloon."

They all burst into laughter.

"As long as the seats don't make my nose bleed and there are no bats hanging in the rafters, I'm good."

* * * * *

One thirty had come and gone, and Matt was still watching for Lucy and Wendy to emerge from the bookstore and meet up with the rest of them in the square at the center of town.

He checked his watch again. 1:57.

Alison and the rest of the group had set out for Joy's Main Street Café, and he was going to wait for the stragglers. Just about the time he thought he might have better luck walking down to the bookstore and dragging them out, he noticed Wendy and Lucy weaving through pedestrian traffic half a block away.

Lucy was beaming and talking a mile a

minute, an overstuffed bag in each hand. It struck him that she had become pretty good friends with her competition, and Matt was happy to see it.

When she spotted him, Lucy lifted her bags and waved her arms, and she and Wendy closed the rest of the distance at a jog.

"I'm sorry; we lost track of the time," Lucy told him. "Where's everyone else?"

"They gave up on you and went down the street to eat."

"But you didn't give up on us," Wendy exclaimed. "You're our hero."

Wendy took one of his arms, Lucy looped the other, and the three of them crossed the street.

"Wait until you see everything I bought," Lucy told him. "We found this darling little vintage shop, and I got an amazing lavender sweater with all this pearl-and-bead detailing on it."

"Oh," Wendy interrupted, "and she found this chocolate parka with faux fur around the hood. It looks so good on her."

"And they had this retro crocheted scarf in a really pretty rust color with lots of fabulous fringe. You should see it with the parka."

Matt raised an eyebrow and stared Lucy down.

"Okay. I get it. Enough."

Turning to Wendy, he said, "This is why God brought the two of you together. I have a limit to how many vintage sweaters and retro scarves I can hear about before the 'overload' alarm goes off."

Wendy's laughter crackled, while Lucy's was sweet like a song. Matt found himself right smack in the middle of something there, and he realized how many years had passed since he'd been privy to this kind of unfiltered interaction between women.

As Lucy and Wendy chattered on about their purchases and then about some romance book they'd both read, Matt meandered along between them, feeling somewhat reminiscent about the days when he used to sneak down the hall and listen outside Lanie's bedroom door for some hint at the intricacies of female thinking. There was a whole other world that women belonged to, and there he was in Mountain View, Arkansas, accidentally knee-deep in it.

"Pay attention!" George would have said if he'd been there. "You're getting a microscopic view into the molecular anatomy of estrogen." George was always hinting at some secret society that existed among the female segment of the population, and he was a true believer in man's ultimate mission to somehow crack the code.

When they reached the restaurant, Matt held open the door for them both. Lucy smiled at him in a way that crinkled her nose.

As she passed him, she said, "Mattie, I'm starving."

"I know. Me, too. Shopping really burns the calories and works up an appetite, doesn't it?"

Lucy giggled in reply.

"We thought we'd lost you three," Alison stated as they joined the others at two large round tables that had been pushed together.

"They were shopping," Matt said, and all of the men nodded, seeming to understand the unspoken.

"What did you buy?" Brenda asked, and Matt knew these four words were sure to bring female-speak to full fruition.

"Look at this," Lucy replied with excitement, pulling the parka out of the bag and slipping into it. "I've been freezing the whole time I've been here. But now—" Producing the scarf, she wrapped it around her neck several times and then modeled it for them all with a dramatic flair. "I will be warm and dry, as well as stylish."

"That is so cute. Where did you get it?" Cyndi asked.

"We found the cutest vintage shop up the street—"

Is this the second or third revisit to the cutest little vintage shop? Matt thought, and he shook his head as he tuned out tales of shopping in favor of focusing on the menu items before him. *The Fireman's Grill sandwich: Ham and Swiss with grilled onions on sourdough.* That looked promising.

A few minutes later, having decided on a *Colossal Kielbasa* sandwich instead, he tuned back in to the conversation at hand.

"This old guy we met on the square

said these are some of the coldest temperatures for October that this area usually sees," Alison told them. "He says we might even see snow in the next day or two."

"Snow!" Lucy exclaimed. "That would be so great. Hey! I could wear my new parka."

"It's not going to snow," Justin corrected.

"Oh, you big old party pooper," Lucy teased. "Don't rain on my snowy parade."

"Fine," he conceded, sharing a cockeyed grin with Tony. "Maybe we'll be able to get some skiing in before we head back."

"Thank you," Lucy said with one firm nod, and she added a little "Humph" just for good measure.

It wasn't the first time that day that Matt noticed the easy way between Lucy and Justin. Matt wondered if she'd actually listened to his advice about being herself, because there was certainly a lightness to her attitude that he hadn't seen since their arrival in Snowball. Even the way she interacted with Wendy signaled a shift in her thinking.

Over lunch, conversations hummed from various points around the table. Alison and Cyndi discussed the local artistry displayed in the café, while Tony, Justin, and Rob conferred about an upcoming Civil War re-enactment they'd seen advertised on the square.

It was then that Matt noticed Jeff and Brenda, their heads close together and their eyes locked, whispering together and looking for all the world as intimate as a couple. Matt was surprised to see it, but he had to acknowledge that they made a pretty good match.

Right at that moment, as if she could read his mind, Lucy elbowed him and shot him a sly grin before nodding in their direction.

"Isn't that great?" she murmured.

"When did it happen?" he asked softly.

"It's been cooking for a while."

Matt should have known that Lucy would be right in the middle of such a development; she loved matchmaking almost as much as the title character of Jane Austen's *Emma*. No one loved a good love story like Lucy Lou, after all.

Matt had often wondered if she would

ever have a love story of her own; but now, the way things appeared to be falling into place with Justin, he expected to find those concerns fully eradicated before too long.

He suddenly realized he'd never taken the time to imagine what would happen to his own relationship with Lucy once she found her match. Somehow, as the speculation began to take hold of him at the big round table in Joy's Main Street Café, he wasn't quite as eager for her to find happiness as he thought he should be.

"Are we all ready?" Alison asked, and the sound of chairs scuffing against the floor answered the question.

"I wish I wasn't so full," Matt heard Lucy say to Wendy as they headed out the door. "Did you see that dessert menu?"

"Peanut butter chiffon pie in a graham cracker crust," Wendy replied, her hand pressed to her heart as she swooned slightly.

"Oh, no no no," Lucy declared. "There was a brownie something. Brownie trumps peanut butter every time."

"Oh, I don't know about that."

"You know, I'm not sure I can be friends with you anymore if you're going to talk like that," Lucy remarked.

"She takes her chocolate very seriously," Matt told Wendy as he took one of Lucy's packages from her full hands. They ambled up the street in several groups, and when they reached the square, Matt noticed that a band of bluegrass musicians had taken their place atop a makeshift stage. There were several banjos and fiddles and oversized basses, and one of the banjo players had a harmonica hooked up to a contraption that allowed him to play both instruments at once.

They joined the gathering crowd, some of them standing, others finding a place to sit wherever they could. Lucy, Matt, Justin, and Wendy shared a long wooden bench to the far side of the square. The musicians were dressed in overalls and jeans, with ball caps and straw hats. Despite the Mayberry-like atmosphere, Matt found it difficult not to surrender to their charm. Before long, he joined the entire audience as they clapped in time to the music and cheered on the performers.

Matt leaned forward and glanced down the bench just in time to see Justin tilt in toward Lucy and say something that made her toss back her hair and break out in unbridled laughter. It occurred to him that they looked very much like a couple, the way Jeff and Brenda had appeared in the café earlier.

Gray clouds whipped around in the steel-blue sky as the late afternoon breeze snapped with a slight chill. Justin helped Lucy slip into her new jacket. She wrapped the long scarf around her own neck, and then around Justin's, as well, with a stream of giggles that traveled down the length of the bench toward Matt.

The bluegrass band announced that they were taking a break, and Alison began rounding up people and herding them off toward the cars. Lucy and Justin followed Jeff and Brenda, and Matt decided to fall back from them a bit and let Lucy enjoy being part of the group's coupled population for a change.

"Hey, that was fun," Wendy exclaimed as she appeared beside him and tapped his arm. "That old guy on the harmonica was a crack-up."

"Did you see that woman in the audience with the hat?" he asked.

"The one with the tag hanging off the back?"

"Yeah."

"Yes! She looked like Minnie Pearl!"

"That's what I was thinking, too."

Matt watched Lucy climb into the back of the PT Cruiser, and by the time he arrived, it was already full.

"Come ride with us," Wendy urged him, and she tugged on his sleeve as she headed for the Buick.

Matt gave Lucy a wave and slid in beside Wendy.

Once they were on their way, Wendy looped her arm into his and gave Matt a smile. "I'm so glad I came on this trip, Matt."

"I am, too."

"I almost didn't come. We were having a festival at the school this weekend, and I didn't want to miss it. But the idea of getting a whole week or more to myself, with adult company and no kids in sight—it was just too compelling."

"I haven't taken a real vacation trip in a couple of years," Matt told her. "So getting a chance to get up here in the fresh air, doing some fishing and some hiking, I just knew it would be a blast."

"Really?" she inquired. "Because I didn't get the idea that you were interested until the very last minute."

"Well, Lucy didn't want to come, and I wasn't sure I wanted to come without her."

"Then I'm really glad she decided to make the trip."

"I am, too," he replied.

The rays of the setting sun turned Wendy's gold hair to a soft tint of orange, and her smile was wide and genuine. In that moment, Matt found himself wondering if he hadn't been overlooking something important in Wendy since they'd met.

Lucy had been in his life for such a long time, and her light was so bright that she consistently outshone every girl who interested him. Her grasp on his heart was as persistent as a bulldog's, and no one else made him laugh or challenged him like his best friend did. He always seemed to end up in the same familiar place with other women, wondering, *Why bother?* But as he glanced at Wendy now, he realized there was something exquisite about her, too. Lucy was a double-shot jolt of pure caffeine. But there was also something to be said for the soothing effect of a creamy mug of English Breakfast tea on a cold autumn morning. Lucy and her tea-loving ways had taught him that.

Maybe he'd have Lucy to thank if this new regard for Wendy turned into something more somewhere down the road.

What a difference a day makes!

Thank You, Lord, for making me realize that forcing myself into a Justin-shaped mold wasn't going to produce a woman he would want. Instead, after my talk with Betty Sue and the things that Mattie contributed, I think You really brought it home for me.

I had the best time with Justin today. There was hardly a break in the conversation from Mountain View all the way back to Snowball today, and for the first time I really feel like we're connecting.

I can hardly wait to see what comes next.

Love and thank You,
Lucy

P.S. And thank You SO MUCH for what's happening with Brenda and Jeff. I've never seen her so happy and content. I think this is really IT for them. High-five for love, Lord Jesus!

Chapter Fourteen

"YOU CAN USE ANY KIND OF MEAT, REALLY. THE healthier version would be ground turkey, but I like a little pizzazz, so I start with a mixture of lean ground beef and some spicy sausage."

Lucy looped her feet through the bars at the bottom of the stool and leaned over the island to watch as Betty Sue used a bright red spatula to mix the meat in the skillet over a low fire.

"Do you want to tend to the pan or chop the vegetables?" Betty Sue asked her, and Lucy reached out and took the spatula. "Okay. Be sure to keep it moving so it just gets browned."

"It's so strange," Lucy commented as she pushed the ground meat around in the pan. "I can't cook a good meal to save my life; never could. But here with you, I really do feel like it's something I can enjoy."

"Finding the right combination of ingredients to make something really tasty is, for me, the ultimate triumph. I never had a daughter to share it with, so having you here in my kitchen, taking an interest in learning my secrets—well, it's nice." After a pause, the older woman asked, "Did you and your mom not spend any time in the kitchen together?"

"I lost my mom to cancer at a young age," Lucy told her. "There were too many things we didn't get to share."

"Oh, sugar, I'm so sorry," Betty Sue cooed as she rounded the island and pulled Lucy into an embrace. When she released her, she smoothed Lucy's hair and gave her a smile. "Maybe you'll come back and visit me every now and then, hmm?"

"I'd really love that."

Lucy's heart expanded with emotion as Betty Sue planted a kiss on the top of her head and returned to the other side of the island to chop the green peppers. For many years, not a day had gone by that Lucy didn't lament growing up without a mother. But as time went on and she grew into a woman herself, she learned to bury that regret. It now reared its head only on occasion.

Meeting and getting to know Betty Sue was a blessing she hadn't expected, and as she tapped the spatula on the side of the skillet, Lucy thanked the Lord for the lovely surprise.

"Okay. Now we'll drain any grease off the meat," Betty Sue told her. "There won't be much because I like to use pretty lean cuts, but just pour it into this colander."

Lucy did as she was told, and she hung on to every word as Betty Sue explained which herbs best complimented the sauce, why she chose that specific mix of vegetables, and how a tablespoon of brown sugar mixed in would cut the acidity of the tomatoes.

"My favorite adventures of this trip have

been the culinary ones," Lucy remarked, shaking her head in surprise. "Whoever would have thought that I was hiding an inner chef?"

"Me. I recognized that in you straightaway."

"I think I've been spending so much time trying to force an interest in things that didn't interest me in the least that I'd forgotten what it felt like to find something that actually stirs up a little excitement inside."

"And cooking does that for you?"

"I'm as surprised as anyone," Lucy told her, "but it does."

"Then here, take this," Betty Sue said, holding out a shiny silver knife with a ten-inch blade. "Chop a couple of onions and have a ball."

Lucy put everything she had into that night's meal, learning all she could from Betty Sue as dinnertime drew closer. The sauce was made from fresh ingredients and homegrown herbs, the mozzarella cheese was grated by hand, and the garlic bread was kneaded and baked right in the kitchen. The only thing out of a box that night was the pasta, and Lucy wasn't sure she could make that claim about another homemade meal in all of her thirty years.

The culmination of the two women's efforts was an enormous pan of cheesy, layered lasagna. Lucy could hardly wait to show the others what she'd accomplished with Betty Sue's tutelage, or to see their faces when they took their first bites.

"I'll slice the garlic bread and get it into the basket," Betty Sue told her. "Do you think you can carry that lasagna? It's very heavy."

"I've got it," Lucy declared, slipping her hands into quilted oven mitts. "I'll come back for the salad."

Lucy pushed through the swinging kitchen door and out into the main room of the lodge bearing the weight of at least ten pounds of lasagna. Games were in full swing, from ping-pong to darts to chess, and her eyes swept through the groups of players to try to locate Justin.

"Is that our supper?" Annie asked her, and Lucy lifted the pan and sidestepped the little girl before she even laid eyes on her.

"Oh, Annie, that was a close one."

"Sorry."

"It's okay. No harm done. Yes, it's our supper. It's Italian Night. Do you like lasagna?"

"I'm not sure. What is it?"

"It's kind of like spaghetti, only it's layered with flat noodles instead of mixed up with skinny ones."

"I like spaghetti."

The pan seemed to be growing heavier in her hands, so Lucy headed toward the banquet table. Just before she reached it, a burst of laughter and cheers drew her attention, and she looked over just as Wendy leaped into Matt's arms and he twirled her around, her legs doing a pirouette in the air.

Before Lucy even knew what was happening, the mitt began to slip from her hand, the handle of the pan she was holding going with it. A fraction of an instant later, the beautiful lasagna she'd worked all afternoon to create went crashing to the ground. Tomato sauce splattered the floor, the tablecloth, and Lucy's pant legs up to the knees.

"Uh-oh," Annie said from behind her.

"Annie!" her mother shouted from the

other side of the lodge. "What did you do?"

"Nothing. It wasn't me, Mama. I didn't do anything, honest."

Lucy covered her face with the oven mitts, smearing tomato sauce across her forehead and into her hair.

"Lucy? Sugar? What happened?" Betty Sue called as she barreled into the room.

Along with everyone else, she fell silent, her mouth gaping open like the swinging kitchen door.

* * * * *

Lucy stepped into the shower, and the embarrassment peaked again as she recalled her excitement about sharing her newfound culinary expertise and the subsequent crashing noise her enthusiasm made as it hit the floor with the lasagna.

"Oh, Lord," she said out loud into the stream of water. "I'm such a dork. Why am I such a *dork*?"

She shook off the sudden reminder that the lasagna had plummeted to the floor after she'd seen Wendy twirling around Matt like a maniac. Their celebration over some great darts move seemed a little over the top. No wonder she'd tossed the lasagna.

"Lucy? Can I get you anything?" Wendy asked through the closed door.

Just some privacy.

"No, thank you."

"All right. Good night, then."

"Good night."

A few minutes later, while she combed through her clean, wet hair, Lucy prayed for forgiveness for being irritated at a person as sweet as Wendy.

"It's been a long time," she whispered upward, "since I've seen another woman with her arms around Mattie. I guess I just freaked out. I know, I know, it's crazy, and I should be happy that he's making a new friend. Wendy might even be a good match for him, Lord. I was just taken by surprise, that's all."

Lucy's hair was still in a towel when she wrapped a second one around her body and opened the bedroom door wide enough to snag her bathrobe from the hook on the back of it. She put a kettle on to boil some water and plopped a tea bag into a mug before wandering back into the bathroom to grab her comb.

She took her cup of tea into the living room and threw open the drapes to reveal a silver slice of moon waiting just outside. She folded up into the corner of the sofa to enjoy it.

"Am I disturbing you?"

Lucy looked up to find Wendy standing just beyond the reach of the frail glow of the lamp.

"Not at all."

"Are you feeling better?"

"Well, I'm cleaner."

Wendy sniggered. "That's always a good start. Can I join you?"

Lucy paused, but only for a moment. "Of course."

Wendy took the opposite end of the sofa, delicately crossing one leg over the other as she angled Lucy's direction.

"The lasagna was great, Lucy."

"Yeah, there's nothing that enhances the flavor of meat sauce like a trip to the floor," Lucy responded, shaking her head and taking a sip of warm tea.

"Stop it. Only a little of it ended up on the floor. The whole tray was still pretty much intact."

Lucy lifted her eyes and stared at her

friend. I don't know if you've noticed this about me, Wendy. I mean, I try to keep it close to the vest. But the truth is . . . I'm an absolute mess."

Wendy laughed. "Aren't we all?"

"N–n–no."

"No?"

"Not *you*."

"Oh, Lucy, you're so wrong. I might not be a mess in the same ways, but I assure you I'm a mess just like everybody else."

"Prove it. I was just about to put on a mint julep cleansing mask. Join me in getting all globbed up and ugly."

Wendy's laughter was melodic. "All right. But no cameras."

"And after that, maybe you could straighten my hair?"

"I'll be glad to, Lucy, but I don't think you'll like it. Those curls of yours are God-given."

"Yeah. He gave them to me just after He graced me with two left feet."

"Hush. Don't be ungrateful. You wouldn't rather go bald, would you?"

Lucy cackled at the thought. "Point taken. Come on into the bathroom and wash your face. I'll get us a couple of headbands and we'll smear our faces with green goo and have some more tea."

"Girls' night in. Maybe we should wake Cyn."

"I say we just spackle a couple of coats of green on her face and let her sleep," Lucy joked.

"You're wicked."

Five minutes later, the women stood side by side in front of the bathroom mirror, their hair pulled back from their faces with terrycloth bands, two big sets of eyes peering out from behind bright neon-green faces.

"And you said you weren't gorgeous, Lucy Binoche," Wendy teased.

Lucy opened her eyes as wide as they would go and contorted her face into a silly grin to reveal teeth and tongue and gums. They both burst into a fit of laughter, and Wendy tried to match the ugly face with one of her own.

"No cameras? Really?" Lucy asked her. "You don't want to preserve this moment with a photo?"

"Do *you*?"

"Absolutely," Lucy joked.

"You're a braver woman than I am,"

Wendy teased back, smearing Lucy's green nose with the tip of her index finger.

"It has to set for thirty minutes. Let's go have some tea and then we'll chisel our way out of here."

The two of them settled on the sofa with cups of tea that Lucy fixed for them.

"This is wonderful," Wendy said, after taking her first sip. "Is there milk in it?"

"Cream," Lucy replied. "At the Conroy, we serve high tea in the afternoons, and we have this wonderful little British lady who does everything in the traditional English way. Including adding cream and sugar to tea, the way Americans do to coffee."

"I've always wanted to try that," Wendy said, and she raised her pinkie as she spoke in her most highbrow English accent. *"Taking tea."*

"You should come down one afternoon for lunch," Lucy suggested. "We'll have cucumber sandwiches and sausage rolls and scones with sweet cream and strawberries."

"That would be such fun. Do they serve the tea in china cups?"

"Yes, and beautiful sterling pots, with Battenberg lace napkins and linen tablecloths," Lucy told her. "And Leslie serves you in this cute little English apron and white gloves."

"Oh, Lucy. I would love to see that."

"We'll plan it, then," she promised.

The creaking of Cyndi's bedroom door announced her entrance, and she sounded drowsy as she asked, "What's going on? Did I miss something?"

Lucy and Wendy both turned around at the same time and looked at her over the back of the couch. Cyndi's eyes grew wide before she let out a long and lingering shriek.

Lucy popped up to her feet. "What?"

Wendy pointed to her own green face and gave an animated grin.

"Oh." Lucy plopped back down to the sofa and started to laugh right along with Wendy. "Sorry, Cyn."

"What is that?"

"Mint julep cleansing mask. Want to join us?"

Cyndi shook her head and turned right back around toward her bedroom.

"Definitely not."

I've learned a lot in the last 24 hours, Lord. I've learned to add a little brown sugar to tomato sauce to cut the acidity. I've learned that your general garden variety of oven mitts actually can be too big for certain hands. And I've learned that, despite my initial efforts not to, I really do like Wendy an awful lot.

It's nearly 1:00 in the morning as I write this, and Wendy and I have spent the last several hours chatting about high tea, stubborn hair, and old boyfriends. I didn't think anything or anyone could make me feel better after the Lasagna Incident, as it will now be known throughout the rest of time. But Wendy really did.

I just don't know what to make of her relationship with Matt. I'd been so concerned about Justin's attention being focused on her that it never occurred to me that Mattie might like her. And I'm not sure why that stunned me the way it did, because the truth is, Wendy and Matt might make a very good match, Lord. Did you already think of that?

Since this is a prayer journal, please hear

my prayer for grace. I don't mean the kind that You've already given that forgives my sins. I mean the kind where I don't trip over my own feet or throw pans of lasagna across the room.

Grace me with grace?

Hopefully,
Lucy

Chapter Fifteen

LUCY COULDN'T HELP IT. FOR THE THREE-dozenth time since she'd awakened, she ran her hands through her hair from roots to tips. She couldn't get over the difference in its appearance since Wendy had used the straightening iron on it the night before. Suddenly she had the silky tresses she'd always dreamed about, at least until the next washing. She could hardly wait for Justin to get a load of her later in the day. For now, however, she would just have to look stunning for herself.

She tightened the belt around the waist

of her bathrobe and picked up her cup of tea. The clock on the microwave read 6:22 a.m., so she determined to tiptoe across the living-room floor in the "Hello Kitty" socks Matt gave her last Christmas as a joke. She was going to let herself out onto the deck while Wendy and Cyndi still slept, eager to enjoy one of her favorite things: hot tea on a cold morning.

She drew back the curtains, unlatched the sliding door, and carefully pulled it open with hardly a sound. The curtain caught on the hand that held her mug of tea, and while she was slipping it loose, she stepped out onto the deck.

Wham!

The bottom of her bright pink socks hit a layer of ice covering the wooden deck, and Lucy went flying in one direction while her tea flew out of the cup and into the other direction. She let out a shriek as her tail end plopped down on the ice. Stunned, she continued to lie there with her hand clinging to an empty mug, her legs spread-eagle, and her mouth gaping open.

So much for that grace prayer being answered speedily.

Lucy looked around her for the first time. The autumn colors that streaked the tree branches the day before were now dusted with snow, and the rolling hills beyond the cabin were glistening white. The gray-blue early morning sky was sifting out large, perfect snowflakes like sugar overtop a tray of cookies.

She leaned her head back and tilted her face toward the sky with closed eyes. As she grinned, flakes fell against her teeth. She stuck out her tongue to catch a few of them and broke into a stream of laughter.

"Lucy? Are you all right?"

She turned to find Wendy standing in the doorway, cinching her robe shut with one hand and extending the other toward Lucy.

"Do you need help?"

"Oh, I'm fine," Lucy told her. "I didn't realize it had snowed overnight, and I slipped on the ice. Isn't it beautiful, Wen?"

"Yes," Wendy said awkwardly. "Can I help you up or something?"

"Oh my goodness!" Cyndi cried as she stepped up beside Wendy. "It's snowing!"

"I know," Lucy cackled. "And Justin said there was no possible way it would."

"Lucy, get up from there," Wendy told her, taking her cup and handing it back to Cyndi. "Come on."

Lucy made it to her feet again and stood with her arms outstretched, letting the snowflakes fall over her.

"I've got to tell Matt!" she exclaimed as she scurried inside and padded across the living-room floor. She snatched up her BlackBerry from the nightstand and plopped down on the bed to begin a text.

"Lucy, you're getting your bed all wet. Change out of that robe first."

"I will. This will just take a second," she replied, *tap-tap-tapping* her message into the device.

Wake up. Look out the window. Meet me halfway.

She dressed in record time and called out to Wendy and Cyndi as she thumped out the front door. "Come on, girls. Come outside!" Half an inch of wet snow was hardly right for a snowman, and there would certainly be no sledding any time soon, but Lucy thought the current conditions were easily ripe for a few snowballs. Wrapped in her new parka and vintage scarf, with only tennies and socks to keep her feet dry, she trekked down the steps of the porch and across the white path that was once a gravel trail.

Lucy crouched near a small drift and began forming snow into a small white ball.

"What are you doing?" Wendy called to her as she made her way down the steps, padded with two sweaters.

"Oh. Just—" Lucy quickly finished packing the snow and turned on Wendy with a huge Cheshire grin. "—this!"

The snowball exploded onto the heart design on the front of Wendy's red sweater, right smack in the center.

"Hey!"

Wendy crouched to form her own hasty snowball, flinging it at Lucy and hitting her squarely on the forehead. Lucy stood for a moment, stunned, and then exploded into laughter.

After a moment, she stopped, gasped for a breath, and narrowed her eyes in disbelief as Cyndi tromped down the stairs with awkward and noisy klunks.

"Hi," she called out to them and then slipped, quickly catching herself on the railing. "Whoa. Uh, hi."

Lucy glanced at Wendy, and they exchanged a look of surprised and silent astonishment before turning back to Cyndi. Her shoes were covered in cropped plastic bags, fastened at the ankles with thick rubber bands.

Lucy's hand sped to cover her mouth as she and Wendy broke out into hysterical guffaws.

"What?" Cyndi asked, clueless. "What are you laughing at?"

Instead of a reply, Lucy hurled a snowball into Cyndi's shoulder, and it sprayed her sour face as it burst.

"Noooo," she whimpered, wiping her cheek with the sleeve of her sweater. "Don't do that."

"Hey!"

They turned to find Matt and Justin headed straight down the incline toward them.

Lucy bridged the distance by running to meet them, hiding the snowball in her icy hand behind her back.

"Isn't it fantastic, Mattie?" she exclaimed,

and then she gently smashed the snow
against his jaw before he had the
opportunity to respond.

Good-natured as always, Matt grinned
as he wiped his wet face. When he was
through, he gave Lucy a sudden and
curious glance.

"What did you do to your hair?"

She pushed the hood down to give him
the full effect. "Wendy straightened it for
me! Isn't it great?"

"Gorgeous," Justin replied. "It really
suits you."

Lucy puffed up as if she had feathers,
and she shot Justin a satisfied smile.

"You," she said, wiggling her index
finger at him. "Mister 'Oh-It's-Not-Going-
to-Snow-You-Silly-Girl.'"

"I know, I know," he said, shaking his
head in surrender. "I bow to your wisdom,
m'lady."

"Well, a girl can't hear *those* words
often enough."

Justin's hazel eyes caught the
reflection of the snow and glimmered like
emeralds. For a moment the sight took
Lucy's breath away. His perfect, chiseled
face gave the impression that he'd been

carved out of stone with great care by a very discriminating Artist.

He placed a hand on Lucy's shoulder, and she tilted her head upward to look into his eyes. A faint, slow smile clung to his lips as he ran a hand through the length of her hair.

"I really like it," he told her with a soft lilt.

"Hmmm?" *Had he said something?*

"Your hair. I really like your hair like this."

"Oh. Thank you."

Lucy's heart beat slowly and steadily, thumping hard against her chest as if pounding its way out with a determined, concentrated effort. The discordant beat of a faster rhythm worked against it in her ears, and she broke the gaze she shared with Justin and looked toward the *tromp-tromp-tromp* of feet against snow-covered gravel.

"Where are you guys going?" she called out to Wendy and Matt as they headed down the hill.

"We're going for a hike before breakfast," Matt returned. "See you at the lodge in a while."

Lucy stood there and watched them, somewhat dazed.

SANDRA D. BRICKER

"Looks like something's happening between those two," Justin commented.

"What?" she asked, looking him squarely in the eye. "What do you mean?"

"Matt and Wendy. They seem to be pairing off lately."

"Do they?"

Lucy's gaze roamed down the trail with them as they wandered away. She could detect the soft hum of their conversation but could not quite make out the words.

"Matt and Wendy?" she remarked. "No. I don't think so."

"They seem like a couple to me."

Matt's just being a good friend, she thought. *Just keeping Wendy busy so I'll have more time with you, silly.*

"Lucy."

His voice was low in his throat, and when she turned toward him, Justin's eyes greeted her with an intensity she hadn't seen before. They narrowed as he smiled at her.

Hey. Wait a minute. Is he about to kiss me here? Is he actually going to ki—

Justin's lips touched Lucy's, soft and warm at first and then with increasing

303

pressure. He touched her face with a soft, gentle stroke before pulling away, and then he came back in for one more quick kiss.

"I've wanted to do that for days," he told her.

"You have?"

Her focus broke away from Justin's eyes for a moment, and she glanced down the hill to find that Matt and Wendy were no longer in sight.

"I have," he replied. "And you were more than worth the wait."

A wide smile stretched across her face, and Lucy leaned in to Justin's embrace, taking one last look over his shoulder and down the hill.

"I'm going to go change clothes before breakfast," she said as she stepped back from the hug.

"I'll see you there, then. In about an hour?"

"Sounds good."

* * * * *

Lucy twisted her straight locks into a knot, tied it into place, and turned on the hot water in the shower.

Wendy and Matt, a couple. Crazy talk.

She couldn't seem to break the stone-faced curiosity stuck to her expression, so she scrubbed it loose with her bare hands. And a little apricot cleanser.

Mattie's not interested in Wendy Marshall, she assured herself. *That is just nuts. I would know if my best friend were falling for someone.*

Lucy produced the body bar she'd brought along in a small plastic container and lathered it up under the spray of hot water. She thought back over the last few years, summoning up quick pictures of the few women Matt had dated in that time.

There was *Shelley the Belly*, the girl with the tightest abdominal muscles in the state of Arkansas. She and Matt were never right for one another.

And then came *Laura the Bore-ah*. All she ever wanted to talk about was the fate of a world that didn't recycle, and after a while, Matt yearned to have a little fun without having to think about how it impacted the planet as a whole.

What was that next girl's name? The one with the fire-red hair and freckles. Sarah? Suzie?

Sabrina.

She had just been too cute to stand, with that high-pitched little voice and a giggle reminiscent of a ride along a very bumpy road.

Wendy was a different story from all of those women, Lucy realized. She was beautiful and smart and funny. She loved the outdoors as much as Matt did, and she could cast a fishing line even better than he could. In fact, Wendy was very nearly perfect in every way, and if Lucy were going to choose a woman for Matt, it was with great reluctance that she admitted to herself that Wendy was an ideal choice.

Matt had, for all intents and purposes, been a big brother to Lucy for as long as she could remember. He was her best friend, after all, and she wanted him to find happiness as much as she wanted to find it for herself.

So why was it upsetting her to think about the fact that he may have stumbled upon *The One* in Wendy? She should be jumping for joy.

Breakfast suddenly seemed like a

chore as a wave of nausea passed through her. But after breakfast, there would be Sunday morning services, and she wasn't about to miss that. Even so, as she put on a little makeup and brushed her silky new hair, all she really wanted to do was lie down for a while.

Hey. Justin Gerard just kissed me! Why am I not walking on air right now?

She was probably just tired, she decided. The day had started early with lots of excitement. A fall on the ice, a snowball war, a first kiss; it was more than she usually experienced in an entire day, and yet it had all occurred before breakfast.

Lucy pressed on. She pulled on a pair of faded jeans and a chocolate cable knit sweater and finished it off with a gold locket on an extra-long chain. It had been a gift from Matt on her last birthday. The cuffs of her new parka were still damp when she slipped into it and pushed up the hood.

The snow had stopped falling, and the morning sky was clear blue against the risen sun. The white blanket laid out over the autumn colors would probably disappear by mid-morning, and Lucy was a little saddened at the realization.

On her way down the hill toward the lodge, she noticed movement just around the curve of the trail. As she approached, she caught sight of Brenda and Jeff, the bright colors of their clothing standing out against the sparkling white scenery. They were locked in an embrace and unaware of anything else around them. Lucy stopped in her tracks, not wanting to interrupt such a tender moment, and her heart soared a bit as they completed the kiss, joined hands, and continued along their oblivious way.

She could almost feel the sweet caress of love in the air as she followed at a distance, and Lucy wondered if Matt and Wendy had paused upon the way of their hike that morning to share a kiss with as much promise as the one she'd just witnessed. If someone had happened upon her and Justin earlier, would they have been captivated or sensed the bloom of new love?

"I don't think I've ever seen you with

straight hair," Alison commented as Lucy stepped into the lodge and pushed back the fur-trimmed hood of her jacket.

"Me neither," she replied. "Just something I thought I'd try."

"Well, it looks nice."

"Thanks, Alison."

Justin greeted her at the coffee buffet, extending an empty mug toward her. "You look beautiful."

And of course you do, too, she thought. But she refrained from saying it out loud. Justin always stood out in a room.

"Thank you," she said instead.

The cinnamon scent of French toast called Lucy to the far side of the buffet, and she placed two slices on a plate and doctored them with butter and syrup. She sensed that Justin was leading her toward a table for two by the window; she wasn't quite sure why, but she pretended not to notice, making her way instead to the longer table where Wendy and Matt were already seated with Cyndi and Rob.

What is wrong with me?

"Good morning," Matt said with a nod. "Again."

"How was your hike?" she asked him, thumping down into the chair next to Matt.

"Oh, it was so great," Wendy answered instead. "That little bit of snow just gave the valley a whole different look and feel. It was so gorgeous, wasn't it, Matt?"

"It really was. I'll be sorry to see it melt away."

"I was just thinking that very thing on my walk down here," Lucy remarked.

"Even if it does melt," Alison said as she joined them, "today's activity is pretty much kaput."

"What was it?" Lucy asked.

"Kayaking," Justin interjected.

"Instead, Betty Sue and Dave have offered to put something together for us this afternoon so we can spend our last day here having some fun and fellowship," Alison announced. "It will be Game Day here in the lodge after lunch. For anyone interested, there will be a Scrabble tournament, dart games, ping-pong, and an array of board games to choose from."

"Fun!" Lucy exclaimed. "Mattie, if they

have any team games, you and I will wash the floor with them."

"It's true," Cyndi chimed in. "It's like they read each other's minds."

"It's freakish, really," Jeff added.

"Let's sign up for one of the teams playing darts," Wendy suggested.

Matt nodded. "Sure. So you can put me to shame."

"So I can teach you how *not* to be put to shame," she corrected, and Lucy looked on as the two of them shared what struck her as a private moment.

"What do you want to sign up for, Lucy?" Justin asked her. "Ping-pong?"

Lucy laughed out loud at the thought. "Not exactly my strong suit."

"Darts?"

"Maybe. I mean, I could try."

"Scrabble?" he said, cringing.

"Now you're talkin'."

"I was afraid you'd say that."

"There are also some Wii games," Dave told them, as he replenished the fruit bowl on the table nearby.

"I love Wii," Justin exclaimed. "Do you have Bowling?"

"Sure do."

"That sounds like fun," Lucy said.

"You're a terrible bowler," Matt reminded her.

"But maybe I'll be better at virtual bowling."

"It's always a possibility. At the very least, it's safer."

"Ha, ha," she mouthed, and then she added, "What other games are there?"

"There's golf, tennis, and ping-pong," Dave replied.

"Maybe you'll be better at virtual ping-pong?" Justin suggested.

Lucy and Matt looked at one another for a moment and said, at exactly the same time, "Doubtful."

Monday — Fishing, bug bites.

Tuesday — Horseback riding. Held my own.

Wednesday — Cooking classes. Couldn't walk after horseback riding. And let's not forget HAY!

Thursday — Underground caverns. Hit in the head by a kamikaze bat.

Friday — Hot air balloon ride. Barfed in front of Justin. Lovely.

Saturday — Mountain View shopping. And of course the Lasagna Incident.

Sunday — Snow! And first kiss with Justin!

It's been such a full week with all the bats and the barfing and the kissing.

Before we came, I joked about leaving Snowball with a boyfriend. And as unlikely as it seemed then, maybe it wasn't a joke at all. But is Matt leaving Snowball with someone at his side, too? Is that what You're doing with him and Wendy? Maybe You decided to put them together so Mattie won't be alone. I guess that's a pretty good plan.

Humbled and grateful,
Lucy B.

Chapter Sixteen

328

LUCY HADN'T REALIZED THAT DAVE WAS A preacher, but he had that comforting, personable quality about him that made him a natural.

"In the Gospel of John, we see that Peter had a certain vision of the way things should go," Dave reminded them from the simple wooden pulpit in front of the blazing fireplace. "When the officers came to arrest Jesus, Peter spontaneously grabbed one of the soldiers' swords and cut off the man's ear with it. He wasn't going to go down without a fight, and this was just not his idea of the way the Son of God was going to be taken. But what do we know from Old Testament teachings? Our ways are simply not God's ways. His thoughts are higher than our thoughts and His ways higher than our ways. Often the way we decide things are going to go are very different from God's actual plan."

Dave taught on the subject of God's will for nearly an hour, and everyone in the room was riveted. Several members of the Bender family were in attendance, along with little fire-haired Annie. The six-year-old wore white tights with a dark green velvet dress and black patent leather Mary Janes. Her wild curls were tamed into long pigtails, held in place by elastic bands with shiny green marbles attached to them. She crinkled up her little nose and waved at Lucy once their eyes met.

Betty Sue stood in front of the wall of glass, looking on. When he was through, Dave thanked everyone for visiting their retreat.

"This place is a little slice of heaven for Betty Sue and me, and we're always grateful when given the opportunity to share it with God's people. Now, we've asked one of our guests to lead us in a song of praise. Wendy, would you come up to the front?"

Lucy's neck snapped as Wendy stepped up, took guitar in hand, and sat on the stool Dave set out for her at the front of the room.

"I'm convinced," she told them all, "that this place is what Dave says it is: a slice of heaven. And for that reason, I thought I'd sing 'Holy Ground.'"

From the moment the first note left her mouth, Wendy had them enthralled. Her voice was as sweet and melodious as any Lucy had ever heard before. She could easily have been a professional.

Lucy looked down the row at Matt, and she noticed that he appeared to be in a trance. He couldn't take his eyes off Wendy, and for that matter, neither could anyone else in the room. Including Justin.

Stop gawking. This is worship time, she reminded herself.

When the song concluded, the entire group of them erupted into sudden applause, and Betty Sue dried her eyes with the corner of a crumpled pink tissue. Wendy thanked them and invited the group to join her as she started "Amazing Grace."

But even as she tried to concentrate on the words of the well-loved hymn, Lucy couldn't resist stealing another glance at Matt. And when she noticed his gaze locked on Wendy, an unfamiliar emotion came over her. She didn't suppose she'd ever seen Matt look at another human being in that way, and it seemed to cut her right through.

This is crazy. What's wrong with me? I should be happy for my friend. Why am I not happy for him? And why am I looking around during praise time at Sunday services?

Lucy closed her eyes for a moment, but when she opened them, she found her gaze locked onto Matt once again.

For crying out loud.

She directed her eyes toward the window, and what she saw outside of it made her blink—and blink again.

"Well, would you just look at that?" Betty Sue suddenly exclaimed as Wendy's song came to a close.

A harmonious hum of wonder filled the room as each person's gaze was drawn out the window, where a blanket of white was coming down like a freshly laundered sheet being shaken out over the landscape.

"The weather report said it would be warming up today," Betty Sue said on a chuckle.

"It almost never snows in these parts so early in the year," Tony informed them, and he scratched his head. "This is just a complete freak of nature."

"Betty Sue, do you have any sleds?" Justin suddenly asked, and a murmur of delight rippled through the group.

"We do," she confirmed. "Three or four of them out there in storage. We can pull them out for you all after services."

"Speaking of which," Dave interjected with a smile, drawing the group's attention back to worship.

Several minutes later, Dave closed in prayer and the group disbursed. Lucy joined Betty Sue in front of the enormous window, and they both watched in silence as the snow continued to fall.

"This is just nuts, isn't it?" Lucy asked. "I've seen tornadoes and rainstorms in October. But has there ever been snow like this?"

Betty Sue wrapped an arm around Lucy's neck and pulled her into an embrace. "I think God mistook us for donuts," she observed, "with all that powdered sugar He's sprinklin'."

A sudden shriek of joy sounded from the hillside, and Betty Sue clamped her hand over her mouth as one of the Bender teens flew by atop a makeshift snowboard. After several seconds, the other two boys followed suit, one seated behind the other on a flattened cardboard box.

"Esther, you're going to want to see this," Betty Sue called out to the matriarch of the clan.

Laughter drew Lucy's attention, and she spotted Wendy and Matt standing together in front of the fireplace. Wendy leaned in toward him and tugged on his sweater, beaming at him like a schoolgirl.

"They sure are getting on well, aren't they?" Alison observed as she stepped up beside Lucy.

"Mmm," Lucy agreed, feigning nonchalance.

"I'm going out to wrangle up those sleds," Dave interrupted, and he gave Lucy a pat on the arm as he passed. "Betty

SANDRA D. BRICKER

Sue, don't we have a box of just-in-casers? Coats and gloves and things?"

"It's on the back shelf," she told him. "I'll come and show you where."

Lucy set out across the room toward Matt, but Justin cut her off at the pass. "Hey, are you up for some sledding?"

"That sounds like fun," she replied and then called out to Matt. "Mattie, let's go sledding."

"It's snowing too hard for sledding," Wendy commented. "I'd rather stay inside, warm and dry, and watch until it stops."

Matt shrugged at Lucy and then smiled. "Warm and dry strikes me fine at the moment. But, uh, are you sure you want to do that, Luce?"

Disappointment pinched her, and Lucy grimaced. "Maybe they're right," she said to Justin. "It is snowing awfully hard out there."

"Are you kidding? This is the perfect time to hit the hills. Come on, we'll have a blast."

Matt had returned to his conversation with Wendy, and Lucy's grimace evolved into a full-fledged frown.

321

"Okay. I'll have to check the just-in-case box and see if there are some gloves I can borrow."

"The what box?"

* * * * *

Matt stepped up to the window alongside a group of others in time to see Dave drag a couple of sleds and a plastic saucer with rope handles out to where the patio would have been if the snow hadn't covered it. Betty Sue followed behind him with a small box and two more saucers.

He watched as Justin zipped up Lucy's parka and tightened the scarf around her neck while she slipped on red mittens that were far too large for her hands.

The minute they were securely in place, she dove for a handful of snow, packed it into a ball, and hurled it at Justin. A full-on war ensued, Justin chasing Lucy over the slope of the yard while Alison, Cyndi, and Rob followed in hot pursuit. It looked like so much fun that Matt, watching from the window, found himself wishing he'd gone with them.

The sky was hazy and gray beyond the

curtain of snow falling from it, and Matt thought that it looked more like dusk than late morning.

"It's beautiful, isn't it?" Wendy asked him, setting down two cups of coffee on a nearby table and nodding him over. "Black?"

"Yes, thanks."

"Lucy and Justin have really found their stride, haven't they?" she asked, and Matt felt a whoosh move through his gut.

"Looks like it."

"I think she really likes him."

"I think so, too."

They watched Justin grab Lucy's hand and drag her toward a sled Matt recognized as a Flexible Flyer. Justin threw it over his shoulder, and he and Lucy hiked across the white carpet and made their way up one of the steep hills.

"You really have a beautiful voice," Matt told her.

"Thanks."

"Have you been singing your whole life?"

"Just about. I was seven the first time I performed in front of our church and ten when I learned to play the guitar."

"I admire that kind of gift. I certainly don't have it."

"Well, it's like the scripture says, each of us has his or her own gifts."

Matt gazed across the table into Wendy's crystal eyes, and the sweetness in her was almost palpable. She was such a beautiful girl, with a heart to match.

"Listen, Matt," she said reaching across the table and taking his hand into hers. "I was wondering if you—"

Matt just happened to glance beyond Wendy and out the window to see Justin hurrying across the snow, Lucy draped over his arms like a sack of potatoes.

"Oh, no," Matt exclaimed, popping up to his feet. "Lucy's hurt."

"What?"

He didn't wait for Wendy, nor did he think to grab for his jacket. Matt just flew out the back door and raced toward them.

Her face and hair were dotted with crystal clumps of snow, and a strange little ice formation in the shape of a miniature dagger was hanging from one eyelash.

"What happened, Luce?"

"My foot," Lucy cried, wincing in pain.

"What happened?" he asked Justin.

"She wanted to steer," he explained. "And she steered us right toward a tree."

"Then I made the very bad decision to try and stop the collision with my foot."

"Ohh," Matt groaned. "That had to hurt. Is it broken?"

"I don't know."

"I don't think so," Justin told him as he carried her into the lodge. "But I couldn't tell anything out there."

Justin set Lucy down on one chair and scraped another in front of her to support her foot. Flicking her scarf from around her neck, he balled it up and placed it like a pillow underneath her ankle.

"Does that hurt?" Justin asked her.

"Only a little."

He began to brush the snow from her hair, but Matt pushed his way past Justin and barked, "Here, stand back." Matt leaned over Lucy's foot and said in a much gentler voice, "I'm going to take your shoe and sock off, okay, Luce?"

"Okay."

"Wendy, would you go find Betty Sue?"

"Sure."

"Justin, get her something hot to drink?"

"Of course."

Lucy let out a screech as Matt removed her shoe, and he wrapped both hands around her ankle protectively. "I'm sorry. I'm sorry."

Matt bit down hard on his lip as he peeled back her sock and eased it away from her swollen foot.

"Can you move it?"

She gasped as she tried and then nodded. "Yeah. It hurts, but I can move it."

"Good. I think that's a good sign."

Betty Sue scurried through the door from the kitchen and rushed to close the gap between them.

"Okay, sugar, tell me what happened."

"I stopped us from running into a tree. With my foot."

"Ouch."

"That's what I said, except louder."

"Did you hear a crack?"

"No. More like a pop."

Betty Sue placed her hand over the swollen part of Lucy's ankle and gave it a gentle press.

"I think it's probably sprained," she told her. "We're going to put some ice on it, and you're going to sit here for a little while. We'll see if it bruises or becomes misshapen. That will tell us a lot."

"Shouldn't we take her to the hospital?" Matt suggested.

"We could, but Dave says the roads are already a mess."

"They are?" Lucy blurted. "How are we supposed to get home in the morning?"

"We'll cross that blizzard when we get stuck in it. Meanwhile, we have enough food stocked up to get us through to Christmas. We have power and heat. We have friends around us, and God's hand beneath us. We're just dandy. Right?"

Lucy nodded, and Matt was relieved when her lips tilted into a grin.

"Okay. I'm going to go get you an icepack. You keep that foot right where it is, and don't dance any jigs before I get back."

"I promise."

Matt dragged a chair next to her and straddled it backwards. "You gave me a pretty good scare when I saw Justin carrying you across the yard."

"Sorry."

"I'm thinking no more outdoor activities

of any kind for you for at least six months."

"Or more," she agreed, her chin angled downward as she raised her eyes and looked at him. "Sorry, Mattie."

"Sorry?" he replied. "You have nothing to be sorry for, Luce. I just thank the Lord you didn't get hurt more seriously."

"We all do," Wendy added.

Matt raked his eyes away from Lucy and toward the sound of Wendy's voice. He hadn't remembered that she was there.

"Here we go," Betty Sue said, and she scuttled toward Lucy with a bright blue cup and a plastic bag of frozen peas. "The peas will stop the swelling, and the hot cider will warm your heart."

Lucy thanked her and stirred the drink with the cinnamon stick poking out of it. She took a sip from the enamel mug and sighed. "Mmm, Betty Sue. This cider of yours is so great. What's in it?"

"Secret family recipe," she told her. "But you're family now, aren't you, sugar?"

Hot Apple Cider (Betty Sue)

1 tbsp. allspice (whole)
1 cinnamon stick
3 cups apple juice
1 cup orange juice
½ sliced lemon
1 tsp. honey
3 tbsp. hot cinnamon candies

Tie allspice into a piece of cheesecloth. Place in a medium saucepan with remaining ingredients. Bring to a boil. Reduce heat and stir, simmering until the candies are dissolved. Remove the spice bag. Stir cider with the cinnamon stick and serve while hot.

Chapter Seventeen

"THE TIN MAN. A CREAKY DOOR."

Lucy's forehead was creased in concentration. Suddenly the crease vanished.

"And old Mrs. Dilson from tenth grade Earth Science! Get it? Things that *need to be oiled!*" she exclaimed, giving Matt a high-five.

"And that's the game," Jeff announced, shaking his head. "Matt and Lucy have won three straight games."

"Who's next?" Matt asked them. "Who wants to be humiliated and virtually slaughtered?"

"I think we should change games," Justin suggested, the slightest hint of irritation detectable.

"You don't like *$20,000 Pyramid*?" Lucy exclaimed. "I love this game!"

"I can see that," he said with a tentative smile.

"Oooh, darts!" Wendy chimed in.

"No one wants to play darts against you, Wen," Cyndi remarked with a chuckle. "We've seen you play."

"Can't we play something that no one excels at?" Brenda said. "Maybe try a level playing field?"

"I'm sorry," Lucy cracked, feigning a very serious expression directed at Matt. "A level playing field? When *we're* in the game? I don't think so."

"Let's break in that Wii game of Dave's," Justin called out, already heading across the length of the lodge before the others began to follow.

"Want a ride over?" Matt asked, nodding toward Lucy's bandaged ankle. "Climb aboard."

He crouched down while Lucy slid to the edge of her chair and wrapped her arms around Matt's neck.

"It's been a lot of years since anyone gave me a piggyback ride," she said on a giggle as Matt provided a smooth and safe transport to the other side of the room.

Wendy pulled a second chair toward Lucy once she was settled, and Alison slipped the scarf pillow beneath her ankle.

"Thanks, gang."

"Need anything?" Matt asked her. "Soda? Snack?"

"Nope. I'm good."

Brad and Sharon Reynolds finished up a game of virtual bowling while the others looked on. But a large, spinning Scrabble board set up on a nearby table drew Lucy's attention, and before long, she had convinced Alison, Rob, and Matt to join her in a game. Esther and her sisters joined the rest of the singles group over coffee, and as their conversation erupted into laughter, Lucy thought how well the two groups fit together.

"Double word score," Alison declared. "That makes it fourteen points."

Matt's grin announced Betty Sue's entrance just before she called out, "Look what I found!"

"What are those for?" Annie asked with excitement as she stomped in the back door, leaving behind two foot-shaped tracks of snow on the floor. "Can I try them out?"

"They're for Lucy. She hurt her ankle," Betty Sue replied as she scurried toward them, a pair of crutches extended over her shoulder like a hobo's sack on a long stick. "These should help you get around a little better."

Rob adjusted them for her, and Lucy took the crutches on a test drive in a circle around the Scrabble table.

"I think if you stay off that foot for a couple of days," Betty Sue told her, "you'll heal much faster."

"Thanks, Betty Sue."

"But I want you to be sure to get an X-ray when you get back to town, all right, sugar?"

"I will."

"Can I try them, Lucy?" Annie asked her when she sat down again.

"I don't think so, sweetie. These are grown-up sized. The last thing we want is your getting hurt on crutches and then needing crutches."

Annie found that hilarious somehow, and her childish laughter reached a place inside Lucy that she hadn't thought about in a very long time. Throughout her twenties, Lucy's primary goal had been to become a mother, but lately she'd started to abandon the idea.

"If you still want another cooking lesson, Lucy, I'm going to start dinner in a while. Would you like to help?"

"I'd love that."

"Can I help, too?" Annie asked them.

"I don't see why not," Betty Sue told her.

"Yaaaaay," the little girl exclaimed, clapping her hands with glee. "What are we having?"

"Oh, all sorts of good things. We'll make some vegetable beef soup, and some dumpling biscuits, and a brisket with broccoli and cheese casserole."

"What's briskets?"

"If your mama says you can help me in the kitchen, you'll find out what a brisket is."

Annie wasted no time at all. She simply turned and took off running toward the door, flung it open, and hollered for her mother.

"Was I ever that enthusiastic about

anything?" Brenda said with a chuckle as she sat down at the table. "I don't think I was."

"Meet you at the kitchen counter in half an hour?" Betty Sue suggested to Lucy.

"Thirty minutes? If I start hobbling now, I might get there by then. Half an hour it is!"

* * * * *

Betty Sue was a champion at setting up a kitchen assembly line. After settling Annie atop a tall barstool with a bowl full of biscuit ingredients to stir with a large wooden spoon, she began piling vegetables in front of Lucy.

"You chop these for the soup while I get the beef in the marinade," she instructed.

Lucy rolled a few zucchinis across the cutting board and picked a knife out of the wooden block. As she chop-chop-chopped, Annie chattered on at breakneck speed, telling her all about her life back in Bellevue, Washington.

"Miss Reesin, that's my teacher, she says I have the knack. That's what she calls being good with numbers. I know almost all my times tables up to the tens, and I can say the fives without even looking. Wanna hear?"

Lucy opened her mouth to reply, but she wasn't given the chance.

"Five, ten, fifteen, twenty, twenty-five, thirty, thirty-five, forty—"

Matt joined in as he walked into the kitchen, and they recited the multiplication tables in two-part harmony.

"—forty-five, fifty, fifty-five . . ." They continued counting until they both shouted in celebration at the end, "one hundred!"

"You know your tables good, too," Annie told him.

"Yep," he replied. "Numbers are my game."

"Hey, mine, too."

Lucy grinned at him as she finished up the zucchinis and moved on to a bowl of bright red tomatoes.

"You wanna do the tens?" Annie asked him.

"Why don't you do them for us," he suggested. "And we'll listen to make sure you're right."

"Okay. Ten, twenty, thirty, forty, fifty . . ."

Betty Sue dragged the bowl of dry

ingredients across the island and finished the mixing on her own. When Annie reached one hundred, they all cheered, and Matt gave her an enthusiastic high-five.

"You rock, Annie," he told her, and the little girl grinned from one ear to the other.

"I know. Miss Reesin says I have the knack."

"Well, she's correct. You really do."

"What kind of numbers do you do, Matt?"

"Oh, all kinds. I'm an accountant. Do you know what that means?"

"Uh-uh," she said, shaking her head, and Lucy thought she'd never seen a more adorable child.

"That means I keep track of all the numbers and dollars and cents for the hotel I work for."

"Is that hard?"

"It can be. But I sure do like it."

Annie turned toward Lucy, tossing her curls over one shoulder. "Do you got the knack, too, Lucy?"

"Not at all," she admitted. "My knack is more about making things pretty and keeping people happy."

"And she does that very well," Matt said, helping himself to a chunk of zucchini from the large green bowl on the counter.

"Is Matt your boyfriend, Lucy?" Annie asked, and all of the adults in the room exchanged glances.

"Um, no. He's my best friend."

"My best friend is Ashley Spriggs. She's a girl. I never heard of somebody having a boy for a best friend."

"I've known Matt since I was a kid," Lucy explained, using both hands to scoop up the chopped tomatoes and return them to the bowl. "He's kinda like a big brother."

Annie leaned across the island with her hands cupping her mouth and said, "I think he's cute."

"Me, too," Lucy said, nodding, and she gave Matt a quick grin.

"Would you wanna be my boyfriend, then?" she asked Matt seriously, her green eyes wide and round and shiny as quarters.

"Well, I don't live anywhere near Washington," he said. "I live in Little Rock. But I could be your long-distance friend. How about that?"

339

"No, thank you. I want a boyfriend."

"I hear ya," Lucy commented without looking up from her chore.

Matt snagged another chunk of zucchini and shrugged one of his shoulders. "You remind me a lot of someone, Annie."

"Yeah? Who?"

"Lucy," he said.

"Honest?"

"Honest. With your long, curly hair and your cute face."

"And we both have some red in our hairs, too."

"I wish I had as much red as you do," Lucy told her. "I think it's very pretty."

"Yeah, I hear that a lot."

They all cracked up at that, but Annie didn't seem to get the joke.

"I do. People always talk about my hair."

"People usually talk about Lucy's hair, too," Matt told her. "But I don't think she really knows how pretty it is. She's always trying to do something to change it."

"Like what?"

"Like straightening it."

"Why would you wanna do that?

People like our curls, Lucy. I think boys do, too."

"Oh," Betty Sue cackled. "People *and* boys, huh?"

"Yeah, Lucy. Don't straighten away your curls anymore. Boys like them," Matt said, and Lucy stuck her tongue out at him and wrinkled up her nose.

"I'm not allowed to do that," Annie announced, and she clicked her tongue at Lucy. "Mama says that's *disrespeckfilled*."

"I think so, too," Matt said with a nod. "Don't be disrespectful, Lucy."

"I'm sorry," she replied for Annie's benefit.

Just as Lucy was about to start on the blue bowl of string beans, Wendy poked her head through the swinging door.

"Matt, we're starting a game of darts. Come on out!"

"Could I watch?" Annie exclaimed, hopping down from her chair, taking Matt by the hand, and dragging him through the door behind Wendy.

"What's your name? My name's Annie," she heard the child ask.

"I'm Wendy."

"Are you Matt's girlfriend?" she asked, and the door swung shut for the final time before Lucy could hear Wendy's reply. She leaned toward the door and strained to listen anyway.

"That little girl is just as sweet as molasses, isn't she?" Betty Sue commented as she took over the child's barstool and began helping Lucy with the green beans.

"She sure is."

But Lucy's heart wasn't into making polite conversation. In fact, she was stuck in the one-track groove of her own thoughts, wondering what was going on between Matt and Wendy. She couldn't help noticing how Matt had perked up the minute Wendy came through the door.

He just about left skid marks on the floor when she asked him to follow her.

"Earth to Lucy."

She blinked hard and looked at Betty Sue.

"I'm sorry. Did you say something?"

"About five minutes of something. You mean to tell me you didn't hear a word of it?"

"I apologize."

"Is it your ankle, sugar? Is it bothering you?"

"Oh, no. In fact, it's feeling a lot better."

"What is it, then?"

Lucy's eyes latched on to Betty Sue's, and she considered confessing the truth about what had her so preoccupied.

"I don't know," she finally said on a sigh, returning her focus to the string beans. "I'm just a little out of sorts."

"Matt and Wendy?"

The knife froze mid-chop, and Lucy lifted her eyes with a slow and deliberate effort.

"What about them?"

"Let me tell you a little story, Lucy. About Dave and me."

"Okay."

"Dave was my brother Vern's best friend when we were growing up. The two of them were inseparable until the time that Vern went away to college and Dave joined the military."

Lucy wondered how this applied to Matt and Wendy. It seemed about as personal to her situation as junk mail addressed to *Occupant*.

"When I knew I wouldn't have Vern as an excuse to see Dave every day, I went into quite a funk. And then one day I realized why."

"Because you loved him."

"Exactly. All of a sudden, I was faced with the idea of not having him in my life all the time."

"I'm not sure how this . . . you know . . ."

"Do you think the funk you're in could have anything to do with the fact that Matt's attentions are elsewhere these days?"

Her first inclination was to deny it, but Lucy couldn't manage it. Instead, she let out a heavy sigh and tilted her head before looking Betty Sue in the eyes.

"I know how selfish it makes me seem."

"I don't think *selfish* is the right word."

"It's just that Mattie's always got my back, you know? And now it seems like I've lost him."

Betty Sue rounded the island and smoothed Lucy's curls with a gentle hand.

"Maybe that's the way he feels about you and Justin, hmm?"

"I guess so."

"And you feel that Justin is the one the Father picked out just for you?"

"Absolutely," Lucy replied in an instant, nodding vehemently.

"Yes?"

Then, for just a moment, she wasn't all that sure about anything anymore. "Well, I thought so."

"Until?"

"I don't know."

"I'll bet you do know."

Lucy's heart was pounding hard, and she was almost too uncomfortable to look at Betty Sue.

"No, I don't," Lucy insisted, and she hopped down from the chair and pulled the crutches into place under her arms. "I'm really tired, Betty Sue. Would you mind if I just go put my foot up and rest for a few minutes?"

"Certainly not. You go ahead, and I'll bring you something warm to drink in a little while."

"Thanks."

Lucy sat down at the first empty table on the other side of the kitchen door, and it felt to her as if she'd hiked a full mile to reach it. She was tired, body and spirit, and it occurred to her in that moment that she hadn't even realized how much her heart was looking forward to going home. Her ivy-draped cottage called to her, from her tiny Tuscan kitchen to her big lumpy bed with the lavender comforter to the brown leather recliner positioned into the ice-blue corner of the living room. The familiarity of it all was calling her home.

At the other end of the massive room, ping-pong balls bounced out their hollow rhythm on two side-by-side tables, and laughter erupted in front of the Wii game.

Matt tossed a dart at the board on the far wall, and it landed very near the middle and the bullseye. When he turned toward Wendy, she wrapped her arms around his neck and drew him into an embrace, and something heavy dropped into the pit of Lucy's stomach.

A fantasy started to burn out of control inside her. She knew she should put the fire out, but she didn't.

I'll just toss the crutches to the floor and take off running across the room. About five feet before I reach her, I'll take a hard leap toward her, wrap my

hands around her neck, and take her down to the floor with me. Then—

Lucy dropped her head into her hands and clamped her eyes shut. "Forgive me, Lord," she whispered. "Forgive me. Forgive me. Forgive me."

"Lucy? Are you crying?"

Her eyes popped open, and Lucy came face to face with six-year-old Annie.

"What?"

"Are you crying?"

"No, sweetie, I'm not crying. I was praying."

"What for?"

"Forgiveness."

"Were you bad?"

"Kinda."

"I know about being bad. It's no good, is it?"

Lucy popped out a single chuckle and shook her head.

"It's really not."

"Nice that God loves us anyway, huh?"

"Very nice."

Right out of nowhere, the little girl leaned forward and wrapped her arms around Lucy's neck and began to pat her on the back.

"It's okay, Lucy. You're not a bad lady. Sometimes good people just do bad stuff."

Lucy twirled her arms around Annie's midsection and lifted her toward her, planting an enthusiastic kiss on her soft, warm cheek.

"I really like you, Annie. You are such a cool kid."

"I know," she replied. "I get that a lot. I like you, too."

Dave drove me back up to the cabin on a snowmobile so I could get some rest and take a shower before dinner, but all I really want to do is go home. At least the snow has finally stopped. That means we'll probably be able to make the trip home tomorrow as planned. As beautiful as Snowball is, I want to head back to Little Rock right this minute, and I don't really know why.

I feel rejected and angry and sad and scared, but I can't really put my finger on what the cause is. I know what Betty Sue thinks. She thinks it's because Mattie's thinking about someone else and I'm not the center of his universe anymore—and I'm such a selfish brat that I'm just not able to deal with that. Is she right? What is wrong with me?

What I really need to do is focus on building things with Justin and let Mattie make his own relationship. I don't want him to be lonely, I really don't. But something inside of me is just rebelling against the idea of him with Wendy.

Help me to get in touch with these

feelings and have control over them, instead of the other way around.

Needing You,
Lucy B.

Chapter Sixteen

Chapter Eighteen

LUCY WAS JUST DABBING ON SOME LIP GLOSS when the expected rap sounded at the front door.

"Be right there, Dave," she called.

One last fluff to her hair and she tucked the tube of iced mocha into her pocket and limped toward the front door. When she tugged it open, she gasped.

"Justin!"

"I borrowed Dave's chariot and came for you myself," he told her, and she couldn't help thinking that the way he grinned at her made him look very much like an actor in a toothpaste commercial. "Are you disappointed?"

"Of course not."

"Hey." Justin looked her up and down and then tilted his head. "Where are those crutches?"

"Oh, I think I'm fine without them."

"Until you get an X-ray, I'm not sure you should take that chance. Where are they?"

"In the hall by the bathroom."

She nodded him in the right direction, and Justin returned a moment later, crutches in hand.

"Ready to go?"

"Ready."

Lucy slipped into her parka and zipped it. As she adjusted the crutches under her arms, Justin lifted her hood and guided her out the front door. Although the stairs had been shoveled and sanded, she was still cautious as she headed toward them.

"Hang on," Justin told her, and he took the crutches from her and dropped them over the side of the stairs.

"What are you—"

Before she could complete the question, Justin lifted her into his arms and carried her down the steps. He carefully set her on the seat of the snowmobile and then went back for the crutches.

"Hold tight," he told her.

When Lucy slid her arms around him, Justin brought his hands to rest overtop hers for a moment, squeezed them, and then turned over the ignition. The spicy scent of him brought back recollections of holiday meals and friendly banter across linen-draped tables, and she couldn't help dropping Justin into the nostalgic seasonal mix. In her mind's eye, there he was, seated at the Binoche family table, passing the pecan stuffing to her father, holding out Aunt Hildie's chair.

It was so cold outside. Pressing her cheek against Justin's back, Lucy closed her eyes and concentrated on keeping her teeth from chattering and her body from shivering to the bone.

She found herself thinking about that first kiss she and Justin had shared on this very trail, wondering why it wasn't more clear in her memory. It should have been the single most important moment of her recent life, and yet she'd spent it wondering about Matt and Wendy.

I hope he kisses me again, she thought as she nuzzled against his jacket for warmth. *Kiss me again, Justin. Give me something to really remember.*

He let up on the acceleration, steered the snowmobile into a shoveled-out opening near the lodge door, and pulled out the key.

"Let me help you," he said as he grabbed the crutches and leaned them against the wall. Justin eased her around toward him and helped her stand. "Careful."

Kiss me again, she thought as she looked up into his hazel eyes. As if she'd issued an audible invitation, he leaned down toward her, pausing just inches away from delivering on her wish.

"Lucy," he whispered just before his lips met hers with a soft, warm touch.

Lucy closed her eyes and enjoyed the kiss with gentle acceptance. When they parted, her eyelids were heavy and slow to open.

Uh-oh.

"Ready to go inside?" he asked her, and Lucy nodded.

Justin slanted the crutches toward her, and Lucy pulled them into place. "Thank you."

He held the door open for her when she reached it, and Lucy grinned at him. But the moment she passed him, the smile evaporated and her face dropped like a burned-out candle.

* * * * *

Matt figured Lucy's pain quotient must be through the roof, judging from the look on her face as she hobbled through the door. He watched as Justin pressed his hand on the center of her back and guided her to a nearby table, helping her take off her parka and folding it over the chair.

Justin leaned down and said something to her, and Lucy nodded before he unwound the scarf from her neck and creased it over his hand before setting it on top of her jacket.

Despite her wounds and traumas, things were certainly working out the way Lucy had hoped. She and Justin had the look of a couple.

Wendy caught Matt's eye and beamed at him.

"Let's check out the buffet table," she suggested, and they closed the gap between themselves and the food that was being set out.

"Betty Sue, you do know how to lay out a spread," Matt told her as he watched her carve slices of beef on a large silver tray.

"This is our last supper together this week," she replied. "I wanted to make it special."

"At least we think it's our last supper," Matt said, glancing out the window at the freshly falling snow.

"Oh, it's started again, Dave," she called out to her husband, and everyone in the room turned toward the wall of glass.

Reactions ran the gamut from oohs and ahs to groans of disappointment.

"How are we going to get back to Little Rock?" Cyndi asked them.

"Let's just see how the weather plays out until morning," Dave advised. "They'll be working through the night to plow Seventy-Four."

"In the meantime," Betty Sue declared,

"let's enjoy supper. Grab a plate and help yourself."

Matt was just about to ask Lucy what she'd like when he spotted Justin hovering over her for the same purpose. When he stepped up to the table and began to dress a dinner plate with Brussels sprouts, Matt touched Justin on the arm.

"Is that for Lucy?"

"Yeah."

"She hates Brussels sprouts. Go with the broccoli."

"Oh. Thanks, man."

Matt coasted through the line and loaded up his own plate. Three slices of brisket; a mound of mashed potatoes and a dipper of gravy; one of Betty Sue's spectacular biscuits; some broccoli and cheese.

"Keep some of the rim free around that plate, Frazier," Justin remarked as he passed. "So you can carry it."

Wendy giggled. "Leave him alone. He's a growing boy."

Matt nodded his appreciation and then planted another biscuit on his plate for good measure.

"Let's take one of the small tables by the window," Wendy suggested. "So we can talk."

Matt followed her and sat down across from her. One of the biscuits fell off his plate as he set it down.

"He may have been right," Matt said on a laugh as he plopped it back onboard.

"Oh, I wouldn't say those words too loud. You never know what you could set into motion by telling Justin that he's right."

Matt loved the way Wendy's blue eyes twinkled when she joked with him. Her pearly white smile set off her eyes even more, and her spun-gold hair formed a perfect frame around her heart-shaped face.

"I've had such a good time this week," Wendy said, as she sliced her food into small pieces. "I just can't tell you how many times I've thanked God that I came."

"It's been a lot of fun. A month's worth of it jammed into one week."

"That's the truth," she agreed.

"I hope the snow lets up so we can get home tomorrow."

"About that."

Matt looked up when she paused. Wendy tried to smile, but it didn't quite make the trip to her face.

"About . . . going home?"

"Well, sort of."

Matt waited for her to expound, but she seemed to be tongue-tied.

"What's up, Wendy?"

"I've been wanting to say something to you," she said, laying her knife and fork to rest across her plate. Folding her hands neatly in her lap, she took a deep breath and expelled it in a slow and deliberate puff. "But every time I've started to, we've been interrupted. Or the time wasn't quite right."

Matt set down his flatware and smiled. "You have my undivided attention now."

"Oh, good," she replied, but he wasn't convinced that she meant it.

"Is something wrong?"

"No," she answered straight out. "No. Not at all."

"Okay."

"Something is right, actually."

"Well, that's good news, isn't it?"

"Matt." She sighed and then looked him in the eye. "I really like you."

"Thanks. I like you, too."

"We have so much in common."

"We do."

"I have such a good time when I'm with you."

Matt considered her words, and then he leaned back against his chair and narrowed his eyes. What in the world was she leading up to?

"And the thing is, when we get back, I would be very interested in going out with you."

He gave his head a slight tilt.

I'm sorry, what?

"You know. If that's something you'd be interested in, too."

Going out.

As her offer began to sink in, a slow and curious smile crept across Matt's whole face. It seemed to comfort Wendy somehow, and she let out a relieved laugh.

"So would you? Be interested in that?"

Matt reached across the table and touched Wendy's hand. "Yes. I think I'd be interested in that."

"You would?"

"I think so," he said with a nod.

"I wasn't sure if you were just being friendly or if you were sensing the connection, too."

"A little of both," he admitted. "I think of you as a great new friend."

"Oh."

"But I'm flattered that you're feeling something more, Wendy."

"I'm so glad."

"You . . . well, you took me by surprise."

"I'm sorry. I've just been trying to say this to you for days."

"Well, I guess I'm pretty clueless."

After a moment, Wendy shrugged. "Yeah. Kind of."

They both laughed at that, and Wendy reached over, picked up Matt's fork, and handed it to him.

"Now that we've got that out on the table, let's eat our supper," she suggested.

Matt stabbed a slice of meat with the fork and nodded at her, trying not to show her the extent of his surprise.

Wendy was a beautiful girl, there was no denying that. It made him the luckiest guy on earth that someone like her would show an interest in him.

Matt allowed his eyes to slide across the room and land on Lucy, where she sat beside Justin at one of the bigger tables. Brenda and Jeff were seated across from them, and they all burst into sudden laughter.

Lucy was getting everything she had wanted to get out of this trip. God had answered her prayers, despite Matt's doubts about Justin being the right kind of guy for her. They looked great together, and they seemed to get along very well; Matt just didn't like the changes Lucy had felt compelled to make in order to set it all into motion.

He looked across the table at Wendy. She pushed back her golden hair over one shoulder and beamed at him as she poked a stem of broccoli with her fork.

"You know," he told her, "when I came on this retreat, a new relationship was really the last thing on my mind."

"I know," she replied. "Same here."

"But getting to know you better has been a pleasure."

"I feel the same way," she said.

"I hope you'll forgive me. I'm a little stunned."

"I understand."

"A gorgeous girl just told me she's interested in dating me. You can imagine my surprise."

"Yeah," she replied, lifting her gaze and let it trace his features. "An unlikely guy like you, getting the girl. That's unheard of. It's a regular *Beauty and the Beast* story."

Matt snorted and tossed his crumpled napkin at her.

"A closed mouth gathers no foot," he said. "Give it a try."

Her laughter rose and fell like the chorus of a song, and Matt shook his head at her as he returned to his dinner.

"Hi, Matt and Wendy."

Annie stood before them, looking very much like a kid in the oatmeal commercial Matt had once seen. She was packaged up in a tufted pink coat and bright purple mittens, and her wayward curls popped out wherever they could from beneath a furry pink hat with flaps over her ears.

"Well, hello, Miss Annie. How are you?"

"Want to build a snowman, Matt?"

"That sounds like a good idea. But I'd

like to finish my dinner. Have you eaten yet?"

"Mmm-hmm," she said with a fervent nod. "I'm all done."

"Tell you what," Matt told her, glancing at his watch. "I'll meet you right out there," and he pointed out the window, just beyond the stone patio, "in fifteen minutes. Okay?"

"Just fifteen, right?"

"Fifteen minutes."

Her little face brightened, and she tried to run away but could only manage a waddle.

"Daddy, I need to have your watch," she shouted, and Wendy and Matt shared a laugh.

"Are you with us?" Matt asked her. "Care to build a snowman?"

"I think not," she said. "I'll watch from inside. I'm not much for the cold and snow."

"You don't know what you're missing. All the creative forces will be at work."

"In twenty-nine degrees. I'll pass."

As he finished up his meal, Matt watched Annie bounce around the room from table to table, rejected by her brother and cousins, hugged by her grandmother, teased by Lucy.

"You know, I think Lucy had that same hat when she was a kid," he told Wendy. Matt wiped his mouth with a napkin, crumpled it and tossed it to his empty plate. "If you'll excuse me, I have a date with a snowman."

"Certainly."

When he reached for his plate, Wendy waved him off. "I've got that. Go play."

Matt took a quick look at his watch and then at Annie, who caught his eye immediately. When she saw him putting on his jacket, she let out a high-pitched squeal and scurried toward him.

"C'mon, c'mon, c'mon, let's go," she said, dragging him out the back door by the hand. "I got you some gloves," she said, tugging two mismatched mittens out of the pocket of her coat. "The snow is really cold on your hands if you don't wear gloves. My mama won't let me in the snow at all without these because it's just too cold."

"I'll bet," he replied with a smile, yanking the small mittens over his large hands.

"If they don't fit, I could go find you some others from the box."

"Nah, I think these will work."

They barely covered the palms of his hands, but she didn't seem to notice.

"Okay. Let's get started. Let's make him really, really tall. Do you know how? Because I've made a lot of snowmans and I can tell you how."

Matt grinned as he watched her pack up a ball of snow with both hands and roll it around on the ground.

"See? Like this. This is how you make it get big."

"Oh. Okay."

"Now you make one."

Before long, they'd drawn a large crowd at the window, and a smaller contingent suited up and came outside to join in the fun.

"You make the bottom one," Ty told Matt and Rob as he began packing his own ball of snow. "Then we can stack this one on top of it. And Annie's will be the head."

Matt looked at Annie. "This is your snowman. Does that sound okay to you?"

Her smile completely took over her

face as she nodded at him. "I think that will work."

In just under an hour's time, the twosome had turned into a group of six, all of them standing back to admire the four-foot figure they'd created. While Alison and Cyndi pushed twig arms into place, Dave provided a bright checkered scarf and a battered Fedora. When Betty Sue arrived with various items from the kitchen, Matt lifted Annie up to create the face herself.

"Maybe the carrot would make a good nose; what do you think?" he asked her, and she nodded as she pushed it into place.

Tony and Dave were quick to catch the head from falling off as she did, and they patted it back into place as Annie dug into the basket for the other features.

She chose a couple of plump prunes for the eyes, and a deep crimson flower created a perfect rosebud mouth.

"What's his name?" Matt asked her, and she snapped back her answer in the flick of an instant.

"Mister Kalamazoo."

"Mister Kalamazoo," Matt repeated, and

he nodded as he appeared to think it over. "That's a pretty great name. Where did you come up with that one?"

"It was just in my head," she replied. "We'll call him Mister Mattie Kalamazoo."

Matt set Annie down so that she could fully admire her work. He happened to glance through the window at the gathering on the other side, and Lucy's was the first eye he caught. She was sitting down, with Justin hovering just behind. She tilted her head and grinned at Matt, her nose crinkled, her eyes sparkling, and a lock of hair twisted around her finger.

Matt wasn't sure he'd ever seen her look so beautiful—or so happy.

Broccoli & Cheese Casserole (Betty Sue)

1 pkg. frozen broccoli cuts
3 eggs
½ cup mayonnaise
1 chopped onion
½ cup grated cheddar cheese
Salt and pepper to taste

Cook the broccoli for about five minutes; drain. Mix together the broccoli, eggs, mayo, onion, and cheese. Add salt and pepper and pour into a greased casserole dish. Bake at 350 degrees for about 40 minutes.

Chapter Nineteen

"WHAT ARE YOU DOING?"

"I'm copying Betty Sue's recipe for that wonderful broccoli casserole she served with the brisket."

Matt lifted the cover of the leather-bound book and chuckled. "Lucy. You're writing recipes in your prayer journal?"

"So I won't lose them. I've got the Sweet Potato Bisque in here, too."

Matt shook his head and sat down across from her as she closed her journal and hooked the pen on the outer binding.

"I think I've learned something new about myself here, Mattie."

"Oh?"

"Yeah," she said, her emerald eyes sparkling with eager excitement. "I think I actually like to cook!"

"Really," he stated. "There's something I never would have guessed."

"I know. Me neither. But meeting Betty Sue has just awakened this whole interest in creating new dishes and trying new things. I mean, Mattie, I was actually thinking I might try to cook something with shrimp when I go home! You know how I love shrimp."

"Have you ever cooked shrimp before, Lucy? You know they're caught out in the Gulf, and they come with eyes and in a shell."

She stuck her tongue out at him playfully and then grinned.

"I hear you can buy them already cleaned so you don't have to look them right in the eye," she said.

"Imagine."

"I know. And someone else actually catches them for you."

"What will they think of next?"

She giggled and flicked his arm with two fingers.

"I've learned something kind of surprising here, too," he told her.

"Really? What is it?"

"It seems Wendy would like to go out with me."

The smile froze on Lucy's face for an instant, and then it melted as she tilted into a shrug.

"Now why would that be surprising?" she asked him. "She'd be crazy *not* to want to go out with you. Anybody would. So you asked her?"

"Not yet. She just told me that she was interested and wondered if I was, too."

"Yeah? So what did you say?"

"I told her I was flattered and a little stunned."

"Oh. So are you? Interested?"

"You don't meet a woman like Wendy very often," he replied.

"That's true. She's pretty extraordinary," Lucy admitted.

"Right. And I think I'd be crazy not to pursue it and see if something's there."

"Are we all ready for our final devotions?" Alison called out, interrupting him. "Let's gather over by the fireplace."

Matt was just about to help Lucy to her

feet and hand her the crutches when Justin swooped in and took over.

"Here you go," he said, removing them from Matt's hands and presenting them to Lucy. "Do you want anything before we head over?"

"Tea would be nice."

"You two go," Matt told them. "I'll get the tea."

"Are you sure?" Lucy asked.

"I was going for coffee anyway."

"Thanks, Frazier."

"You bet."

Matt watched them walk away, Lucy on her crutches and Justin with his hand planted on the small of her back.

At the buffet table, Wendy handed him one of the two coffee cups in her hands.

* * * * *

"'There is no fear in love,'" Rob read from his Bible. He pushed his wavy, dark hair off his forehead and looked up at them. "That's in First John, chapter four. 'There is no fear in love; but perfect love casts out fear, because fear involves torment.'"

Lucy thought about how glad she was that Rob was presenting the devotions, because she hadn't really had the opportunity to get to know him very well. These lessons were always a pretty good insight into people.

"Torment is a great word for it, too," he continued. "I'm thirty-six this year, and I've been tormented a good bit about reaching an age where so many of my friends and colleagues have already married and started their families."

Lucy counted forward on the calendar inside her head. Just a few more weeks and she would be thirty. She understood Rob's concerns all too well.

"It's so easy to give in to fear on that subject, isn't it? We get into our thirties and we start to worry. Time marches on, like it's bound to do, and worry becomes anxiety. Anxiety becomes fear. And fear, as the Word says, involves torment."

A little flutter in Lucy's stomach gave way to a fury of butterfly wings, flapping around inside of her.

"If I've learned anything in my thirty-six years," Rob told them, "it's that we tend to make foolish choices when we're operating in fear. Fear is a very destructive enemy. It leaves hurting and angry people in its wake. And so I think it behooves us, as singles, to take hold of the Word and believe in that perfect love that casts out fear. Don't latch on to the wrong person out of fear that the right one will never come along.

Anxiety swooshed through Lucy's stomach, and an unexpected mist of emotion rose in her eyes.

"My grandmother used to say, 'Desperation makes for bad bedfellows,'" Rob said on a laugh. "She was a very wise woman, I think."

"My aunt Sue told me that it's better to be alone than to marry the wrong man," Alison piped up. "I've always believed that to be true."

There were many nods and murmurs of agreement from the group, and Lucy noticed a look pass between Brenda and Jeff, followed by mutual smiles. Jeff reached over and took Brenda's hand into his.

Lucy remained silent, her hands folded in her lap and her eyes cast downward as she mulled over all that she'd just heard. She wondered if Rob's message had been sent just for her.

She glanced over and met Justin's

gaze, which told her he'd been waiting for her to do so. Another wave of anxiety crested and left Lucy feeling queasy.

"So in closing, I'd like to read you this passage out of First Corinthians, chapter thirteen, from the NIV. If God chooses to bless us with partners, let this be the way we choose them, without haste and without fear.

"'Love is patient, love is kind,'" he read. "'It does not envy, it does not boast, it is not proud. It is not rude, it is not self-seeking, it is not easily angered, it keeps no record of wrongs. Love does not delight in evil but rejoices with the truth. It always protects, always trusts, always hopes, always perseveres. Love never fails.'"

Deep down in her gut, Lucy felt that there truly was a takeaway message for her in tonight's devotions. The verses from First Corinthians played over and over in her head, cementing her conviction about their significance.

Lucy knew a love that was patient and kind, never proud or self-seeking, one that kept no record of wrongs, that protected, hoped, and never failed. Yes, the love of her Father was every bit of that and more. But there was another love in her life that stood up to the scrutiny of every point in the passage of scripture Rob had just read.

Justin smiled at her just then, and she returned it, filtering out the sadness as best she could.

But it's not you, Justin. You're not The One.

* * * * *

Lucy propped her feet on the coffee table and fluffed her hair. She identified the exact moment when doubt started to creep its way into certainty. It was just as her second kiss with Justin had come to a conclusion.

It was strange that their first kiss had been so unmemorable, but she'd chalked it up to the fact that she had been distracted by Matt and Wendy. But she'd prayed for their second kiss, wished it into being, yearned for the jolt of chemistry to make it unforgettable.

But Lucy had felt nothing. Not even a small glimmer of zeal that she could coax into the vicinity of passion. As handsome and funny and personable as Justin was, when he kissed her, the magic just wasn't there.

What a letdown, she thought. *He has it all.*

And then there was that one little thing. He wasn't Matt.

Lucy wondered why it had taken her so many years to realize the truth. She'd known him since she wore knee socks, for crying out loud. He'd seen her through the devastation of losing her mom, the disenchantment of countless relationships; he'd even sat on a hard plastic chair in her hospital room for two days when her appendix had burst and the infection had her out of her head.

For richer or for poorer, in sickness and in health, for better or for worse.

It was at that moment that Lucy fully realized what a remarkable husband Matt would make. At what point had she decided to see him solely as the brother of her best friend and later as her own best friend? When had Matt's kindness and humor and appeal been draped with this dreadful cloak of denial? She wondered if there was one specific day or a single fateful moment when her future happiness had been stabbed to death by the appalling dagger of her own defiance.

What have I done, she asked herself now as she waited for Justin to come back from the kitchen. *Lord, what have I done?*

"Okay. This is hot, so be careful."

As Justin handed her a mug of coffee, Lucy decided to set Matt aside for the time being and focus on how in the world to tell the man before her that she wasn't interested in pursuing a relationship.

"I'm so glad you invited me in when I brought you back," Justin told her as he sat down beside her on the sofa. "We so seldom get any time together, just the two of us. And I was hoping to talk to you about where we go from here."

There came that queasiness again.

"Well, Justin, I'm interested in discussing that, too," she began. "I don't really know how to say this to you."

"You don't have to say it," he said, taking her hand. "I think I feel the same way you do, Lucy."

"I don't think so."

"Honestly, I do."

"Justin. You don't."

He tipped his head curiously and narrowed his eyes at her. "I don't?"

"No. I'm sorry, but you don't."

"I don't understand."

"Justin, this is all my fault," she said. "You are such a wonderful guy, and when I started to get to know you, I thought God had done something really amazing by bringing you into my life at just this time."

"See. That's how I feel, too."

"But the thing is . . . just because you're handsome and funny and wonderful . . . well . . . that doesn't automatically mean that you're the right guy for me."

He winced. "It doesn't."

"No. And I'm so sorry about it, too. Frankly, I've been working my tail off to convince you that I'd be the right woman for you, and the truth is, I'm not."

"But we have so much in common, Lucy."

"Do we? Because I don't think we do."

"We have our faith."

"Yes. We have that."

"And we both love the outdoors."

"Right there," she said, tapping her finger on his hand. "The outdoors. The thing is, I'm not really an outdoorsy type of girl."

"But you—"

"Justin, I went fishing, and I wanted to hurl. I went on a hot air balloon ride, and I actually did hurl! I don't really like horses except from a distance, and small, confined spaces like those caverns you crawled around in make me want to scream and pull out all my hair. The only things I've really enjoyed about the outdoors on this whole trip were the s'mores."

Justin laughed at that and then lowered his eyes and fell silent.

"Snowball. It's a good name for this place," she said softly. "Not just because of the freak snowstorm, but because I haven't been showing you my true self, Justin. I've been showing you someone who doesn't exist, and those efforts have been snowballing out of control ever since we arrived."

"Why?" he asked her. "Why did you feel like you had to do that?"

"Well, I blame you," she stated, and she broke into a full grin. "You're so

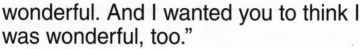

wonderful. And I wanted you to think I was wonderful, too."

"I do."

"But you've only seen the version of me that I wanted to show you. The real me? I would much rather camp out in a four-poster bed at a five-star hotel than out here in the great outdoors. If I'm going to ride a horse, it's going to be in the carriage it's pulling. And Justin, I hate wearing tennis shoes every day. I'm one of those peculiar girls who actually feels more comfortable in a pair of heels. I'm a true girly girl, Justin."

"Really?" he asked.

"Really," she said with a nod. "I miss my four-hundred-thread-count sheets and my Egyptian cotton comforter more than I can possibly explain to you. I'm just not the woman I led you to believe I am. And I'm so sorry. Please forgive me."

"You know," he told her thoughtfully, "I saw all that when we first met. You know, that you were a little too *femme* for my usual taste. But you just impressed me so much with your willingness to try anything, even when you were obviously failing miserably."

Lucy let out a laugh at that. She hadn't realized he knew just how miserable her failures were!

"And when I kissed you, I just—"

There's no need to bring up the kiss! Please don't make me tell you that it didn't cut the mustard. Pleeeeease.

"—really thought there was something going on between us. It seemed like you were feeling it, too."

In what hemisphere?

"Oh, Justin. I'm sorry." It was all she could think of to say. "Forgive me?"

After a long moment of consideration, he nodded. "Of course."

"Thank you. I hope we can still be friends."

He fell back against the couch, clutching an imaginary arrow in his heart.

"I know, I know," she said on a giggle. "But I really mean it. I do want to be your friend."

He rose up again and gave her a smile. "It couldn't have been easy to say the things you've just said, Lucy."

"Well, no. It wasn't," she replied.

"I appreciate your candor. I don't like it. But I appreciate it."

Father, please forgive me. And help me.

No matter how hard I look at it or from which angle, I can't for the life of me figure out what caused me to pursue Justin like a bloodhound after a fox. Well, probably because he is a fox. And that makes me feel incredibly shallow.

This whole week I've been willfully ignoring a nagging feeling deep down inside. And if I've learned anything in my life, it's that we can't make good decisions solely based on emotion. Or on physical attraction and butterflies in the stomach.

I guess the bigger issue at the moment is the realization that You had already brought me someone who meets all the criteria You set out in Your Word about what love is, and I looked right past him. For years, I haven't seen the blessing that You set out before me. Really, what is wrong with my vision?

As I listened to Rob read from First Corinthians, Your words formed a sudden lightning bolt that shot straight into my heart. There was no "feeling" or "emotions" about it. Just certainty and assurance. And now I know that I know that I know. I love Matt, and it's too late.

What have I done?

Please help me to stay out of Matt's way. He deserves to find love. He deserves to be happy. He said to me, "You don't meet a girl like Wendy very often," and he's right. She's extraordinary. She's everything I would wish for Matt, except, of course, for the fact that she's not me.

Looking at it from every conceivable direction, it's so clear to me that I came to this realization about my own heart just a week too late, and I have no one to blame but myself. That crushes me. But even though it seems unbearably unfair to me, I can't overlook the fact that it would also be unfair to Matt and Wendy for me to speak up now and rock the whole boat.

So I'm going to do something that doesn't come easily or naturally to me. I'm going to shut up and see what happens.

It's the right thing to do. But not the easy thing. Please help me. My heart feels extremely fragile right now, like one good sneeze could shatter it and blow it all away.

The thought of Matt finding someone

else just when I feel like I've found him . . .
it aches. It just aches.

> Not enjoying the pain so much,
> Lucy

Chapter Twenty

LUCY WIGGLED HER ANKLE UNDER THE COVERS, stretching it first in one direction and then in the other. Poking it out from under the blanket, she lifted her leg up in the air and held it there. The swelling in her ankle had gone down considerably, and it wasn't as sore as it had been.

When she heard the front door to the cabin swing open, she kicked her way back under the blankets and flopped over on her side to face the wall. Burying her head into the pillows, she clamped her eyes shut. Then she remembered that the lamp was still on, so she rolled over again, flipped it off, and tossed herself back to her side.

Her heart pounded. *Bump-bump-bump-bump.* She willed it to quiet down as she laid there pretending to be asleep. Just as it started to comply, she heard Wendy and Matt whispering on the other side of the door, and the thumping revved up again. Her heartbeat was so loud in her own ears that she couldn't make out what they were saying or if they were saying anything at all.

She realized that she was holding her eyes shut with such force that she was creating tiny fireworks in the darkness behind her lids. As she struggled to relax, she imagined what was going on out there in the silence that screamed at her from the other side of the door. The sparklers returned as she tried to shield herself from visions of soft caresses and tender kisses.

Stop it, stop it, stop it, she repeated to herself, but Matt and Wendy burned the insides of her eyes.

The front door thumped shut, and the switch of the yellow lamp clicked. Lucy strained to hear faint footsteps padding across the floor on the other side of the door just before it creaked open.

"Lucy? Are you awake?"

She held her breath until Wendy sighed and closed the door behind her. Fabric swooshed, shoes klunked gently to the floor, and blankets ruffled until Lucy felt certain that Wendy had settled into bed. Delicate hints of white flowers and citrus made their way throughout the room, and Lucy made a mental note to check the perfume bottle on the bathroom sink in the morning to find out what mellifluous scent Wendy wore. It reminded her of summer, even in the middle of an autumn snowfall.

Lucy forced her thoughts elsewhere. She wondered about Lois back at the Conroy, how the Leary wedding had gone, whether the caterer had remembered to keep cilantro out of the menu. At last she heard Wendy's breathing grow deeper, and she waited for several more minutes just to make sure. Then, with as much care as she could muster, she slid out from beneath the covers and planted her feet into the slippers that waited on the floor next to the bed.

Sans crutches, Lucy limped a little as she crossed the bedroom. She grabbed her bathrobe from the hook and gently eased out into the living room, closing the door behind her.

She pulled back the drapes and peered out into the dark night. Cupping her hands against the glass, she tried to see if it was snowing again. It didn't look like it, but she couldn't tell for sure. After a moment, she lifted a chair from its spot in the living room and set it down in front of the window. Drawing her knees upward, Lucy circled her legs with both arms, rested her chin on her knee, and stared out into the darkness.

It's going to be a very long night, she thought. *But tomorrow, I get to go back home.*

* * * * *

What's new. R u back yet.

Matt read the text from George and hit reply.

Back later today, weather permitting. Will call.

A voice mail from Lanie told him she was stuck in Chicago: "Isn't it too early for this kind of snow? You have no idea how cold it is here."

Oh, I have some idea, he thought as he snapped his watch into place and zipped up his jacket before heading out the door.

Matt saw his breath in a thick cloud before him as he crunched along the snow-carpeted path down the hill to the girls' cabin. The steps up to the door were slick, and icicles hung in tapered formation from overhead like spiky decorations. He was careful not to knock too hard so they wouldn't fall.

"Morning, Matthew," Wendy said with a wide grin when she opened the door. "Can you come in for just a second?"

"Sure."

Matt stepped just inside the door while Wendy layered a couple of sweaters on top of one another.

"I sure do wish I'd brought a coat," she told him as she buttoned the last one. "I'm padded enough to play a game of football."

"I think you look cute," he replied. "Like the Sta-Puff Marshmallow Girl."

"Just the look I was going for."

She picked up her bag from the counter and then placed a hand on Matt's shoulder and gave him a peck on his cheek.

"I'm starving," she said.

"Where's Lucy?" he asked. "Should we wait for her?"

"She was already gone when I got out of the shower this morning."

"Really," he stated. "That's so unlike her."

"Probably meeting Justin."

"No, he's still sacked out."

"Hmm," she said, "I don't know then." She broke into a wide smile. "Let's go eat breakfast."

Matt noticed the crutches leaning against the wall by the bedroom door. "She couldn't have gone too far," he said, pointing them out.

"Oh, you're right. Ready to go?"

Matt nodded, and he followed Wendy through the front door.

"Watch your step," he told her. "It's slippery."

Wendy reached out for his hand and then held on to it all the way down the hill to the lodge as she entertained him with accounts of her students and the art class she'd taught a few weeks prior.

"I've never been away from class this long before. I didn't anticipate missing the kids as much as I do."

"I'll bet they can hardly wait for you to get back."

"Well, I think that's true, but only because Mrs. Donnelly is the substitute, and she's a little strict for my preschool crowd."

Wendy's laughter was melodious, and Matt found himself feeling a little sympathetic toward the kids in her class. If he'd had a teacher like Wendy in his youth, he might have developed into a far more attentive student.

The minute they walked through the front door, Matt heard Lucy's voice from the kitchen.

"Coffee," Wendy sang, pointing at the table and heading straight for it.

"Go ahead," Matt told her. "I'll be right there."

Poking his head through the swinging door, he found Betty Sue and Lucy at the island, Lucy's face and clothes dusted with a layer of flour as she used a wooden spoon to kick up a cloud of it from a huge porcelain bowl.

"I see it's been snowing inside, too," he teased, and Lucy looked up at him with weepy eyes. "What in the world are you doing to Betty Sue's kitchen?"

"Girl talk and pancakes," Betty Sue answered for her.

Lucy wiped her nose with a corner of her apron and then grinned at Matt. "Banana and blueberry pancakes, with homemade macadamia nut syrup."

"Good grief."

"I know."

"Need some help?"

"No boys allowed in my kitchen," Betty Sue told him. "Now skedaddle."

Matt raised both hands in surrender and retreated backward through the swinging door. The picture of Lucy covered in flour stayed with him, and he found himself grinning as he closed the space between himself and the table where everyone was gathering.

Wendy was already seated, and Brenda, Jeff, Alison, and Rob were there as well.

"Hot and black," Wendy said as she slid a mug of coffee toward him. "Just how you like it."

"Thanks," he said and then turned his attention toward Alison. "So what's on the schedule today? Any chance we're going to get home as planned?"

"I think so," she replied. "Dave suggested waiting until late morning so there's time for the roads to be cleared and for the sun to help that along, but I think we'll all be home in time for supper."

"Great. I'm expected at a meeting of all the financial geeks tomorrow morning. And I'm the head geek."

Wendy giggled at that, and they shared a smile.

"Is it my imagination, or is there something going on between you two?" Brenda asked, straight-out.

Wendy colored and looked at Matt. "Well, we're getting to know each other better, and we'll see what comes of that."

Matt watched Wendy look away, and he thought how adorable she came off while being discreet.

"How about you and Jeff?" Wendy

countered playfully. "It sure seems like you two are pairing off."

The laughter that followed was fraught with expectation from the group. Matt wondered how Brenda would respond.

"Touché," she said, and nothing more.

"Bren's just bitter," Jeff told Wendy, "because she foresaw you pairing off with Justin. And she just hates to be proven wrong. About anything."

Brenda chuckled and nodded. "True enough."

"Hey, here comes Lucy with a breakfast tray," Rob announced. "Let's place bets on whether it makes it to the table."

"Rob, that's just mean," Cyndi reprimanded him, and Matt was glad that she did.

Shaking his head, Matt got up from the table and headed toward Lucy. He reached her as she placed the tray of scrambled eggs into the chafing dish.

"Your foot must be better," he said as he reached her. "You left your crutches behind."

"Yeah, once the swelling went down, I didn't really need—"

"Luuuuu-ceeeeee."

They both turned to find Annie running toward them, and Lucy crouched down just as the little girl reached her and threw herself into her arms.

"Good morning, you," Lucy sang. "How are you today?"

"I'm good. I didn't sleep too long and I was up before everybody. Mama says I beat the sun up this morning. So she made me some hot chocolate and we played Go Fish! Did you ever play that? It's a card game and you ask for a card and if the person doesn't have it, you say, 'Nope. Go Fish!'"

"I have played that," Lucy told her, and she glanced at Matt with a smile. "It was one of my favorite games when I was your size."

"I like that one, and I like Old Maid, and I like to play Sorry, too. Did you ever play Sorry?"

"I'm not sure."

"I like that one," Matt remarked.

"I'm always the red player," Annie told him. "What color are you?"

"I'm partial to green."

"Annie, leave those folks alone and

come over here," Esther called to her granddaughter and then waved at Matt and Lucy. "She'll talk your ear off if you let her."

"They don't mind," Annie said with confidence. "They like me, dontcha?"

"We do. You're right," Lucy replied.

"Come over here right now, Annabelle."

"Uh-oh," Annie said. "When she calls me that, I know I better pay attention."

Lucy cracked up at that, and she ruffled Annie's hair before the girl ran off to join her family.

"She's so cute I get a toothache," Matt told her. "She's a little Mini-You."

"I give you a toothache?"

"Not so much anymore, no," he replied seriously, and Lucy smacked him on the arm as he guffawed. "But you used to be very sweet."

"You stinker," she said, shaking her head as she turned back toward the kitchen. "No pancakes for you."

"Hey, do you need some help?"

"Nah. Betty Sue and I have it."

Matt watched her disappear and then poured himself a glass of orange juice. He looked up from the table as Justin blew through the front door, his clothes disheveled and his hair uncombed and falling down into his face.

"What's up with you?" Matt asked him, as Justin poured a cup of coffee. "Wake up on the wrong side of the Ozarks?"

"You have no idea."

"Well, what is it? What happened?"

"Zilch," he groaned. "Absolutely nothing."

It seemed to Matt like the whole place froze the instant that Lucy and Betty Sue came through the kitchen door loaded down with breakfast trays. Justin's eyes met Lucy's, and sirens sounded off.

Lucy broke the gaze first, following Betty Sue to the banquet table, and Matt watched Justin pull himself together before he trailed them.

"Hey," he heard Justin say to Lucy, and she smiled tentatively.

"Hey."

"How are you doing?" he asked.

"All right. You?"

Matt heard Justin sigh and say something that sounded like, "I've been better." But what followed was spoken in hushed tones. Something had obviously occurred between the two of them, and Matt wondered why Lucy hadn't shared it with him.

A moment later, Lucy whispered something and Justin nodded in reply, and the two of them embraced. Whatever the issue was, it had apparently been resolved.

Matt drained his orange juice glass and smacked it down on the table just as Betty Sue called everyone to breakfast.

"At last!" he exclaimed. "Let's eat."

Matt spooned out a heaping serving of eggs and stabbed a couple of pancakes from the platter.

"Be sure to try the syrup in the blue pitcher," Lucy suggested. "We made it from scratch."

This side of Lucy surprised Matt. She was as excited about that cinnamon macadamia syrup in the blue, flowered pitcher as she'd been about anything else he could think of. He dipped his finger into the syrup that puddled around his pancakes, tasted it, and gave Lucy a quick double take.

"Are you kidding me? You made this?"

"She sure did," Betty Sue exclaimed.

"Betty Sue is a great teacher," Lucy told them. "She's totally inspired me. I'm even thinking about taking some cooking classes when we get home."

Matt shook his head as a laugh burst out of him. "Chef Lucy Lou. Who knew?"

"Well, after we enjoy Chef Lucy's lovely breakfast," Alison announced, "we can all start packing our things and get ready to check out of our cabins. We'll meet at the cars in two hours." Checking her watch, she nodded. "At eleven a.m."

"Check!" Tony exclaimed.

"Maybe there will be time to hike up to the ridge one last time," Wendy suggested to Matt, and he nodded.

He'd been hoping for the chance to get Wendy alone before they set out for Little Rock.

The bad news: I discovered the love of my life about twenty seconds too late.

The good news: Mattie will always be in my life. He's my best friend.

I'm a walking, breathing, tragic love story. The only thing that would make it more of a made-for-TV movie would be if I'd contracted a rare, disfiguring disease while feeding starving children in the African jungle and was sputtering out my final breath when I discovered the truth at last.

"Cough. *Oh, Mattie.* Cough. *Have a beautiful life with* (cough) *Wendy and your six amazing, blond children.* Cough. *Be happy. And never forget* (cough) *that I* (cough) *love you.*"

I'm a soap opera.

Will he marry her, Lord? Will I one day be the Best (wo)Man at his wedding, forced to smile until my cheeks ache while I watch him pledge his undying love as he slips a platinum eternity band on her finger next to the princess-cut, two-carat engagement ring that he gave her at the stroke of midnight on New Year's Eve?

Because that would really stink.

So anyway . . . I packed my bags and

then spent some time out on the deck to write a thank-you note to Betty Sue. Five minutes after I curled up with my journal on the bed, Wendy floated in.

As I write this, she is in the room with me, folding her clothes into neat little squares that she stacks in her suitcase like chips in a Pringles can. Who does that? Who is that meticulous?

She certainly doesn't look as happy as I would look if I'd just won Mattie's heart. But then she doesn't know him well enough yet to know what a wonderful guy she just scored.

They stole away after breakfast for a last romantic walk along the ridge, while I sat in the kitchen with Betty Sue crying my eyes out.

She's such a good woman for listening and sympathizing and telling me things like how You're the One in control and how if Mattie and I were truly meant to be, then this will only be a hiccup in getting there. I'm pretty sure we both knew that Matt and Wendy are a no-brainer and the chances of him finding his way to me after being with her are slim to none. But it was very kind of her anyhow.

I just want to take this time to thank You for bringing me to my senses and stopping me before I made a full commitment to a pretty face just because he was there. Don't get me wrong. It hurts like salt on a scraped knee to know I'll never get to tell Mattie what I finally figured out about myself and my heart. But at the same time, I'm grateful that You didn't let me snowball my trip to Snowball any further than I already had.

I hope You'll find someone lovely for Justin, because he's a very nice man. He's just not MY very nice man. Mattie is.

What am I supposed to do with THAT, I wonder.

Slow but sure,
Lucy Louise Binoche

Chapter Twenty-One

Chapter Twenty-One

LUCY FOLDED HER JOURNAL SHUT AND CLIPPED her favorite pen on the binding before sliding it into the outside pocket of her bag.

"I guess that's it for me," she said. "I'm ready to go. How about you?"

Wendy had her back to Lucy as she leaned over her suitcase and zipped it shut. She didn't turn around when she replied, "Almost."

"Do you want to walk down together?"

"No, you go ahead. I'll catch up."

Lucy slipped into her jacket and tugged at the zipper. Just as she was about to yank her bag off the bed, she glanced Wendy's way and did a double take.

"Wen?"

Wendy was perched on the corner of her bed, silent tears cascading down her cheeks.

"What is it?" Lucy asked, and she sat down next to her friend, slipping an arm around her shoulder. "Are you all right?"

"Oh, I'm fine. Go ahead down to the cars," she sniffed. "I'll be there in a couple of minutes."

"Wendy, I'm not going anywhere until you tell me why you're crying."

"I can't tell you, Lucy."

"Of course you can."

"No. I can't. Please just go. I just need to wash my face and pull myself together a little."

Lucy looked at her friend long and hard, and Wendy nodded at her.

"Are you sure?"

"Yes, I'm sure."

Lucy stood up and smoothed her jacket before crossing to her own bed and picking up her bags.

"Can I get you anything?" she asked.

"No. Thank you, though."

She carried her things out the door and across the living room, but Wendy's red, weepy eyes stayed with her somehow, and Lucy couldn't bring herself to leave without providing some sort of comfort or support. She stood for a full minute with her hand on the doorknob, debating about what to do and wondering what could have happened to make Wendy so upset. For a moment, she considered going to get Matt to see if he could help, but then she realized perhaps he'd been the one to say or do something to cause the disappointment in Wendy's blue eyes. Men could be so clueless sometimes.

"Wendy," she said as she stepped back into the bedroom. "I can't just leave when you're like this. Please tell me what's wrong. Did Mattie do something dumb because—"

When Wendy didn't lift her head, Lucy hurried toward her and gingerly sat down beside her.

"—because men can be so thoughtless, and I'm sure he didn't mean whatever he said or did."

Wendy surprised her when she looked

up and smiled at Lucy through the mist in her eyes.

"Yes, he did, Lucy. He meant it."

"Lanie used to have this T-shirt that she would wear all the time, Wendy. I wish I had it right now, because I'd give it to you to wear home. On the front it said, 'BOYS ARE STUPID.'"

Wendy laughed, wiping her eyes with the back of her hand.

"Whatever Matt might have said or done—"

"Lucy," Wendy interrupted, pressing her hand firmly against her leg. "Matt wasn't stupid or clueless. He just doesn't want to go out with me."

"Yes, he does."

"No. He doesn't."

"He told me himself," Lucy insisted. "He said women like you don't come along every day. He said he'd be a fool not to pursue it and see where it would go."

"Yep," she nodded. "He told me all of that, too—"

"Then what makes you think—"

"—right before he added that he just didn't see us going anywhere."

Lucy pinned down the pop of glee the minute it reared its head.

"Wendy, that doesn't make any sense at all."

"Well, that's what I thought, too," she said, and she pressed her lips together for a moment. "Until he told me about the extenuating circumstances."

"What circumstances?"

"I really don't think I should go into that, Lucy."

"What do you mean? I'm Mattie's best friend. If there were extenuating circumstances, I think I would know what they are. Are you sure you didn't misunderstand what he was saying?"

Wendy giggled and then smiled sweetly at Lucy. "No, I didn't misunderstand."

"Do you want me to go have a talk with him? Because I think he needs to clear this up between you before it gets—"

"Lucy," Wendy said, exasperated. Taking one of Lucy's hands between both of hers, she added, "Matt is a wonderful guy, and he wanted to be completely honest with me so that I didn't end up getting hurt. I appreciated that very much, even though I didn't like what he had to say."

"I don't understand."

"Matt has feelings for someone else."

"He . . . What? No, he doesn't."

"Oh, Lucy. I think everyone knows it except the two of you."

"Knows what?"

Lucy's pulse was racing, but her senses were caught in a fog of molasses and she couldn't break free.

"Lucy. Matt is in love . . . *with you*."

An invisible fist socked her right in the stomach, knocking the wind right out of her. She tried and tried, but she couldn't seem to catch her breath.

"I shouldn't be the one to tell you this. Matt should be the one," Wendy told her, but the words were lost beneath a monotone hum in Lucy's ears. "But I don't know if he'll ever tell you, Lucy. And if you have even the remotest idea that you might love him, too—"

"I do!" she exclaimed, and then she clamped her hand over her mouth, astonished.

"You do?"

"I do," she said through closed fingers.

Wendy gently lifted Lucy's hand from her mouth and held it. "You love Matt?" she asked her.

Before she could answer, Lucy popped to her feet and stood there like a stunned deer caught in the headlights of an oncoming semi truck.

"Lucy?"

"I love him," she declared without blinking. "I love Matt."

Wendy tugged at her wrist, pulling Lucy around to face her. She looked at Lucy so hard that the weight of it pressed her down.

"He's on the ridge," Wendy stated. "Go tell him."

Lucy's feet were stuck in concrete, and her heartbeat burned in her chest as it bounced around violently.

"Lucy. Go tell him."

Their eyes met, and Lucy was desperate to read something in Wendy's eyes that would clear the haze and help her to understand.

"Go," Wendy said, and the key turned in Lucy's ignition at last.

First she jumped from one foot to the other and then let out a tiny squeal.

Wendy grinned and nodded, urging her on, and Lucy sprinted toward the door on the power of sheer adrenaline. In the doorway, she turned back and met Wendy's eyes again.

"Really?"

"Really."

"Should I—"

"Go!"

A million scenarios bumped into one another in her head, and Lucy couldn't make heads or tails of any of them except for one brief moment of unexpected clarity.

She turned back and looked at Wendy through a mist of emotion in her eyes.

"Wendy?"

"Go," she repeated.

"I'm so sorry."

"No," she said, shaking her head. "You have nothing to be sorry for, and neither does Matt. But don't fumble this, Lucy. Go to him and make it right. Tell him the truth, and let him tell you."

Lucy clutched at her heart with both hands. She tried to find her voice, but it was nowhere to be found, so she formed the words with her mouth.

"Thank you."

Before she could think about what she was doing, Lucy was out the door and down the stairs, limping up the hill as fast as she could.

Rob called to her from the front door of the men's cabin as he dragged his suitcase across the threshold, and Lucy's ankle throbbed as she slipped to a stop.

"Matt?" she asked him. "Is he inside?"

"No, he's still out on a hike with Wendy, I think. Up on the ridge."

Snow and gravel flew as she sprinted up the trail, past the other cabins, and over the top of the hill. And suddenly, there he was.

Matt.

Seated on a boulder with his back to her, staring out over the edge of the ridge, postured forward and leaning on his knees.

"Mattie," she said softly, and he didn't move a muscle.

She stepped closer, slowly, and her final footstep caught his attention as she crunched through several inches of ice and snow. He turned around and looked at her, his eyes squinted against the sunlight.

"Hey, Luce. What's up?"

"You love me?" she asked without thinking.

"Well, of course," he said, and then realization dawned and his face melted down to embarrassment. "Wendy told you what I said?"

Lucy nodded emphatically, stamped her good foot, and repeated, "Mattie. You love me?"

Matt pushed up from the boulder and faced her, burying his hands deep into the pockets of his jeans. His wavy hair fell across his forehead, and he looked up at her awkwardly from beneath it.

"Luce."

"Mattie, answer me! Do you love me?"

But before he could reply, that final stomp of her foot broke through a thin layer of ice, and Lucy screamed as she grabbed for a tree branch and missed, flying several feet down the slope of the hill until she thudded to a stop, buried to her waist in a drift of snow.

"Oh . . . my . . . goodness . . ."

"Hang on, Luce. Hang on."

Matt hopped over the drift and crouched down behind Lucy. Grabbing her under the arms, he started to pull upward.

"Ouch! You're breaking me in half," she cried.

"I'm not breaking you. I'm saving you."

"Well, could you save me a little more gently, please?"

Matt propped his foot against the tree trunk for traction and then let loose with a fierce groan as he pulled Lucy up and out of the snow.

She laid out, flat on her back as she tried to catch her breath, with Matt standing over her. He extended his hand toward her, but she just glared up at him.

"So did you say it, Matt? Did you say you loved me?"

He let his hand flop back to his side and growled. "I can't believe Wendy told you that."

"You're right!" Lucy felt a bit like a Chihuahua on a slick linoleum floor as she struggled to get her bearings and make it to her feet. When she finally did, she repeated, "You're right, Mattie. She shouldn't have told me. *You* should have told me."

With that, she began brushing the ice

421

and snow off of her jeans and jacket. When she was just about finished, she faced Matt and tilted her head into a lopsided shrug.

"Why didn't you ever tell me?"

Matt sighed. "I don't know. I didn't want to ruin everything between us."

"How would it be ruined?"

"Well, you'd feel all awkward, and be like, 'Oh great, this poor guy's carrying a torch for me,' and nothing would be the same between us because of it."

"What if I'm carrying a torch, too?"

Matt considered her words and then looked away. "That's not funny."

"No. You're right. It's the *unfunniest* thing I ever realized about myself, Mattie. When I thought I was in love completely alone, it was torture."

Matt grimaced. "What are you saying?"

"I love you, too, Mattie."

"Since when?" he asked, skepticism lurching from beneath his expression.

"Since ever, I guess," she admitted. "But then I kissed Justin and realized there wasn't a single spark of attraction beneath it, after all that build-up . . . and then Rob read that verse out of First

Corinthians about all the things that love is and isn't—"

"Wait, what was that about kissing Justin?"

"I felt nothing, Mattie. Nothing at all."

"Maybe it was a fluke."

"It wasn't, because I tried again."

"And?"

"Nothing."

"Are you sure?"

"I think I'd know if I felt something or not, Matt."

"And you didn't."

"Nope."

Matt seemed to be thinking that over, and then he moved toward her, scooped her up by the waist, and pulled her close to him. First, he smiled, and it warmed her from the top of her head to the slope of her swollen ankle. And then he moved in closer.

His lips were soft and hot, and when they touched hers, Lucy felt an ember crackling somewhere inside of her. Without any warning at all, the fire spread, and it enveloped her until Lucy actually heard herself moan softly and felt her knees go weak. Without Matt's arm around her waist, she knew she would have fallen right back into the snow.

When he pulled away, he raised an eyebrow and grinned.

"Anything?"

"Oh yeah."

"You're sure?"

"Uh-huh."

"Let's try again," he whispered. "Just so there is no mistake."

Lucy thought she heard music somewhere in the distance as he kissed her again, but she forgot all about it as the butterflies in her stomach took flight, their wings fluttering against her insides.

"We've wasted so much time," she told him, her eyes still closed, her head tilted backward and draped over his hand.

"Shh," Matt said softly. "We're here now."

"Thank God for Wendy," she replied on a giggle as she opened her eyes and looked at Matt.

"Thank God Himself," he declared, and he moved in and kissed her again.

"Stop it," she said when they parted. "I can't breathe. You make me not breathe."

Lucy's heart was pounding so hard that

she was certain Matt could hear it. Tiny crystals of snow fluttered downward from her lashes when she blinked, and she closed her eyes tight and leaned into his embrace.

"I love you so much," she whispered.

"Lucy, I love you, too."

"I don't know how I could have missed it all these years."

"I know what you mean."

"Kiss me again, Mattie?"

"I thought you needed to breathe."

"I did. Now I'm ready for you to take my breath away again."

Epilogue

I can't believe I'm here, Lord.

It's six months to the day since I stood on that ridge outside and told Mattie how I felt about him and he told me that he loved me, too. Now I'm just hours away from marrying him on that very ridge, wearing the princess-cut platinum ring that he placed on my finger, while down on one knee, at the stroke of midnight on New Year's Eve. And it only took us a couple of decades to get here! I always did like to take the scenic route.

It's amazing how things have worked out, isn't it? I asked Wendy to be a bridesmaid, and George Sedgewick is the Best Man . . . and while we've been planning a wedding, the two of them have been falling in love! Whoever would have thought that a pretty girl and a couple of visits to church could turn George's whole life around this way? George has committed himself to You, and in a few months he'll commit to Wendy. Only You could do that. I love that about You.

Lanie got in last night, and she and Wendy and I sat around in this cabin drinking tea and munching on Oreos, giggling like schoolgirls while we gave each other manicures and painted our nails. It was such fun.

Annie and her mom should be arriving in a few hours. I can't wait for her to see the frilly pink flower girl dress I have for her!

In a few minutes, I'll go and wake the girls so we can be ready when Betty Sue brings us breakfast. And then they'll all help me with my hair and makeup and get me into my beautiful, antique, ivory silk taffeta gown with ruching and glass-bead accents. It's the dress of my dreams. And Matt is the man of my dreams.

You know, it suddenly hit me like a ton of

bricks in the middle of the night, but I was thinking that Lanie and Justin might make a pretty great couple. What do You think? They'll both be at the wedding today. It couldn't hurt to do a little suggesting, right? I'm usually pretty great at spotting a natural couple like the two of them.

Aside from the whole thing about taking decades to realize Mattie was The One, of course.

On second thought, maybe I'll just let You do the matchmaking from now on. You seem to have a pretty good handle on that.

All matched up and happy,
Lucy ~~Binoche~~ Frazier

P.S. One last recipe for my prayer journal, Lord. And this one I concocted all on my own . . . with Your help, of course.

A Happy Life

2 cups each of understanding, love, and encouragement
1 Tbsp. pure extract of trust and loyalty
1 pinch humility
2 mustard seeds of faith
1 gallon concentrated prayer

Stir together and simmer over a low heat.

Add one best friend that you can't live without and garnish with humor to taste.

Serves two, for life.